That which is unshakable with the test of time is truth, what falls apart is myth.
– Aniruddha

SYSTEMA PARADOXA

ACCOUNTS OF CRYPTOZOOLOGICAL IMPORT

VOLUME 09
EYES OF THE WOLF
A TALE OF EL CADEJO

AS ACCOUNTED BY ROBERT E. WATERS

NEOPARADOXA
Pennsville, NJ
2022

PUBLISHED BY
NeoParadoxa
A division of eSpec Books
PO Box 242
Pennsville, NJ 08070
www.especbooks.com

ISBN: 978-1-949691-69-6
ISBN (ebook): 978-1-949691-68-9

Interior Design: Danielle McPhail
www.sidhenadaire.com

Cover Art: Jason Whitley
Cover Design: Mike and Danielle McPhail, McP Digital Graphics
Interior Illustration: Jason Whitley

Copyediting: Greg Schauer and John L. French

DEDICATION

To Stephen King, whose Holly Gibney was the inspiration for my Chimalis Burton.

Prologue

El Salvador, 1845

The old magician watched the two boys draw closer to his home as the hot sun began to set. *Most odd*, he thought, because it had been years since anyone as young and as vibrant as these two had tried to find him, and so far off the natural path. He could only surmise that they were trying to seek him out. For what purpose, he did not know, but he would learn soon enough.

He stepped through a drape of bleached bird and rodent skulls stitched together with dried pig sinew and greeted them warmly. He lifted his equally dry arm, a narrow tree branch of sagging black skin, and reached out to them with long fingers knotted and twisted by years of systematic abuse at the hands of his master. That was many years ago when he had been a slave in Belize, but the scars from that time still lingered in his body, mind, and spirit.

"I greet you," he said, his voice a mix of pebbles and uncontrollable phlegm. "I am Zaka, and I welcome you to my home."

Zaka could see that the boys were young, sixteen or seventeen at most. They were not African like him, but rather, a mixture of Spanish blood and either Xinca or Alaguilac, based on their features. They were streaked with soot and greasy grime far darker than their skin. Their clothing was dirty, worn, and threadbare. A light, sparkling gold dust covered them from head to toe. The gold dust gave them an air of importance, but the old magician knew the truth: they were just simple boys far from home, and perhaps, lost?

"Hola," the one closest to the magician said. "I am Miguel. This is my brother, Isai. We are from the gold mines south. We are on our way home to celebrate our sister's marriage, but we were robbed of our food and mule as we traveled. We have a long way to go, and we are tired and hungry. We were wondering if…"

The boy paused, looking at his brother for support. Isai finished. "We were wondering if you could give us food and a place to sleep for the night."

"Really?" Zaka said, surprised and more than a little impressed by these brave young men who would dare approach his home. "Do you know who I am? *What* I am?"

Miguel nodded and swallowed. Zaka could hear and see the boy's throat move despite his weak vision and the cataract clouding his left eye. "We have heard rumors, yes. You are a magician, they say, and you make fetishes and love potions and boil frogs and lizards and rats to make—"

"—to make potions to raise the dead," Isai interrupted, "and poisons to subdue or kill the wicked."

"Now, now, now," Zaka said, moving his hands as if he were trying to stifle a growing argument. "Those are all just silly, childish rumors perpetrated by the Spanish and their European masters to discredit and embarrass me. Yes, I do make potions and fetishes, but not just for love or death or other trivial matters. Orisha of the Yoruba charges me to help people like you, like me, travel through their life free from harm, from persecution." He motioned to the thick forest around him, glorifying in its splendor. "I can protect you as you walk through these forests from the mines to your home or to anywhere you wish to go. I can provide you amulets that will protect you as you make your way through life, forever and for all time. But… I do require payment."

"We don't have any money," Isai said, his expression turning foul. "We just told you we were robbed."

"Isai," Miguel barked, then shied away at his brother's glare. "Show some manners, please."

"But he wants us to pay, and we—"

"I did not say that you had to pay with coins," the old magician said. "I said merely that you had to pay. Payment can come in many forms."

The brothers waited, and Zaka continued. "I will give you food and rest, and I will gift you two amulets to protect you in your travels if you agree to one simple task."

The boys looked at each other, then nodded.

"I am old, you see." The magician chuckled. "These days, I have barely enough strength to lift a feather, but I require wood for my fireplace. If you agree to gather wood for me before you leave in the morning, I will humbly admit you into my home and allow you to avail yourself of my hospitality. Do you agree?"

There was a long pause. Miguel and Isai looked at each other. "Very well," Miguel said finally. "We agree."

"It is very important that you understand this agreement and keep it. I will take your word as your bond. If you violate my trust in—"

"We agree!" Isai barked. "You have my word."

Zaka nodded. "Very well. Please, come in."

So they entered the magician's home, carefully navigating through a jungle of hanging bones and drying red peppers, onions and roots, and strings of beads that appeared to have been dipped in blood, and small feather fetishes with the dried, leathery faces of rats and squirrels. At the center of the small house stood a table. There was a loaf of brown bread there twisted in knots, and the brothers sat and ate greedily. To wash it down, Zaka gave them bowls of thick, soupy wine.

The boys ate and drank far into the night, and as they did so, Zaka made sure he let the middle finger of his right hand draw across a part of their skin as he served them their food and drink. From this, he was able to divine each boy's true nature.

Miguel was a relatively good boy, well-mannered, courteous. He was younger than Isai by two years. He was easy to manipulate emotionally, and sometimes his older brother took advantage. Isai was brash, bold, prone to anger, and not always trustworthy. They each had warm feelings for the other, though it was difficult to express such emotions openly. Isai especially, for he was the oldest and destined to be the man of the house one day. It would not do to show outward weakness, for doing so allowed others to take advantage.

Interesting, Zaka thought as the evening's conversation and feasting came to a close. *Let's play a game.*

Miguel rose to go outside and gather the firewood as promised. Zaka waved him off. "Please, it is late, and there are beasts in the forest that will make a meal out of you at this hour. Come, rest by the fire, and in the morning, you can fulfill your promise."

The boys did as Zaka said. They took comfortable places by the fire and quickly fell asleep.

As the boys slept, Zaka placed the rest of his bread and wine on the table. He then quickly made them two amulets from copper infused with small bones from the tody motmot. Then he, too, fell asleep.

In the morning, he heard voices.

Isai's first, in a harsh whisper. "Come on! Grab the food, and let's go."

Then Miguel. "What about the amulets?"

"Forget them. Just get the food and come on."

"We promised to get him wood for—"

"Forget the old man. He's crazy, senile, and he won't be able to catch us anyway. Come on!"

Miguel gave in to his brother, as Zaka had expected, though that saddened him. He had hoped that Miguel would finally show strength and stand up for himself, stand up for what was right, to keep the promise that he and his brother had made. Zaka kept his eyes shut, however, until Miguel grabbed up the food with a deep sigh and followed his brother out of the house.

Zaka rose. He looked at his table. The food was gone, but the amulets remained. He looked at his withered pile of firewood. No resupply.

He walked outside and saw the boys trotting down the path in the rising glow of the sun, both laughing. He shook his head.

He closed his eyes and raised his right arm, and through his pebbled, watery voice, said, "I curse you both for your discourtesy. I condemn you both for stealing, for lying, for breaking your promise. I curse you, Isai, for your blatant disrespect and evil tendencies. I curse you, Miguel, poor young Miguel, for your lack of courage. I pray that in time, you will both find a better path on which to walk. But until that day, may you walk this earth in fear and pain, in confusion and sorrow. I curse you in the name of Orisha."

The brothers halted immediately, dropping their stolen food. They fell to the ground screaming. Then they began to change.

Their limbs were replaced by long, grey-and-black furred legs like a wolf, but instead of claws and large paws at the ends, they grew hooves like the goat. The flesh of their chests and stomachs peeled off in chunks of bloody skin and were replaced by thick canine fur and muscle. Their necks grew longer, stronger. Their faces bulged into muzzles filled with sharp, yellow-white fangs. Tiny horns grew on the top of their heads.

The change took only a few minutes, and at the end, terrifying howls replaced their human screams and pleas for mercy, echoing in the rising sunlight. When the transformation ended, they sniffed and scraped at the thick, sticky remains of their human bodies littering the path. They seemed confused. Turning to face Zaka in their wolf-goat forms, they howled in such a way as to frighten even him. He braced for an assault.

Instead, they growled and scratched at the path as if charging, and then they bolted away, off the path and into the deep, dark forest.

They were gone, and the old magician waited until their howls dispersed with distance.

Zaka breathed a sigh of relief. He went back into his house, grabbed his walking cane and his broad-brimmed hat, and carefully walked down the path to retrieve his discarded food.

He never saw the two boys again.

CHAPTER ONE

Javier Torres was a new border patrol agent, but he was no fool. He understood his duty and the safety protocols required of his position. So, when Dispatch ordered him to investigate an apparently abandoned eighteen-wheeler just a few miles past the border checkpoint south of Laredo, he called for backup. An abandoned semi on a dark highway near the Mexican border was nothing to take lightly in his line of work. But this one didn't seem so worrisome, so dangerous. Something about it seemed inviting, almost welcoming, and it called to him.

Torres pulled a flashlight from his glove compartment, flicked it on, and stepped out of the car. He approached the semi from behind, moving slowly in the bright high beams, casting his long, dark shadow against the chained double-wide rear swing doors.

The truck was a standard Peterbilt, heavily worn from constantly moving back and forth across the US-Mexican border. Parked with care off the highway. Hazard lights on, but faint. Engine on. The smell of diesel fumes annoyed Torres' nostrils as he rubbed his face while moving closer. "Odd for the doors to be chained," he mumbled to himself. "Very odd."

He moved toward the driver's side of the truck. Nothing odd or out of place with anything along the length of the trailer. No structural damage, save for a couple of small gashes in the trailer body; not uncommon. Wheels were good; no visible flats or punctures. Nothing leaking. Nothing to indicate any mechanical problems that might have forced the truck driver to pull over.

Look in the cab…

Torres obeyed the persistent whisper in his mind. He un-snapped his holster and placed his hand on his revolver. It always gave him pride to do so. He, young Javier Torres, once an un-documented boy who had crossed the border with his parents fifteen years ago, now a citizen entrusted with a gun and bor-der protection of the United States. It gave him chills thinking about it.

As he drew closer, the high-pitched voice of male singer Ozuna singing *Taki-Taki* blared over the cab's radio. He cared for neither the song nor the beat. These days, he was more interested in country musicians like Chris Stapleton.

"Anyone in the cab?" he shouted, loud and distinct over the music and rumble of the semi's engine. "Put your hands through the open window and state your name!"

He repeated the order in Spanish. No one complied.

Torres drew his pistol and held it forward with the flashlight. Calling out a third time, he inched toward the door. He shined his light on the door handle while putting his foot on the cab's step, careful to keep his pistol trained on the door. He then reached for the door handle and opened it.

The driver of the truck spilled out of the cab, his face bloody, his throat cut. His thick, meaty frame plopped onto the road in a sloppy tangle of body hair and disheveled clothing.

Torres holstered his pistol, pulled his radio from his belt, and called for backup again. "Officer Javier Torres requesting backup. I have a male driver down. I repeat, I have a… middle-aged, male truck driver down at—"

Come now… come and see…

The voice in his mind was strong. Like his own voice, with a touch of accent, but old, bitter, unrepentant, and persistent. Unforgiving, angry.

He tucked away his radio, grew silent, and looked at the trailer again.

What was inside the truck? It could be a number of things. It could be nothing more than innocent, innocuous imported (and perhaps, illegal) goods from Mexico, just like thousands of other trucks that rolled across the border and through Laredo on any given day. It could be empty, or…

He dared not say what he suspected. That, too, was not uncommon. *But the driver…* He decided not to check the man to see if he was dead. Checking vitals in such a situation was standard practice for officers, but something about the way the man had fallen out of the cab, the way his head had hit the pavement, the indiscriminate crack of his neck, the gross slosh of the corpse in its own blood and waste upon impact, told the truth. The man was dead. Were the contents of his truck dead as well?

Torres placed his ear against the box. He heard and felt nothing save for the hum of the engine. He waited a moment, showing patience to ensure no sounds. He tapped his fist on the side to see if he could rouse anyone inside. Nothing.

I've got to see for myself. He didn't want to, and unless there was a clear sign that anyone was in the truck, he was to wait for that damned backup taking too long to arrive. But that stubborn voice whispered to him again, deep inside his mind. It rose up into his thoughts like boiling water in a teapot.

Open the door… open the door… come and see…

Torres returned to his car and grabbed his bolt cutters. He went to the back of the truck and placed them on the chains that held the door shut. He snapped the links quickly.

Torres swung the doors open. Something sprang from the darkness of the box and struck him down.

His body slammed against the pavement. The immediacy and shock of the strike dislodged his bolt cutters. He reached for them, but the beast in his line of vision and the headlight glow of his patrol car gave him pause.

A wolf, larger than any wolf he had ever seen. Its deep red eyes were fixed on his face, pulsating like the hazard lights of a truck. Its muzzle and teeth were slick with blood, and its dark tongue hung out panting and dripping bile. Torres reached for his holster and pistol, but the beast put its paw — no, its hoof — on his hand as if they were greeting each other in kindness.

Turn from me, it said in the deep recesses of Officer Torres' mind… *look away… or die…*

He did as the beast ordered. Behind him, Torres heard the *clop-clop-clop* of the creature's hooves as it scampered away into the quiet night.

Its voice faded from his mind, and in its place, madness grew.

Aspen, Colorado

The Atasaya rose before Chimalis Burton. A hulking brute seven feet tall. All muscle, spattered blood, and dense bone, it tore itself out of its current form of a small, demure old lady and stood before her like a Zuni god. More like a Zuni demon, in fact, as it beckoned her forward with large hands knotted in red knuckles sporting tiny horns that squirted green ooze. It mocked her with a maw of sharp yellow teeth and tusks.

Come to me… come to me, and I will give you peace.

Chimalis ignored the beast's call and instead lunged toward it with a knife, blade sharp and ready. The symbols of previous demons that she and the knife had vanquished together glowed red hot along the hilt of the blade, and that gave her courage to fight hard for her life.

Then everything changed. She no longer had the blade in her hand. The beast now feasted on her legs, grinding bone and muscle as it worked its way up toward her crotch. Slurping her flesh like she were a roasted chicken, muscles tearing, her bones cracking like brittle glass. She tried beating the beast away with tiny fists. Nothing. It just kept eating and laughing, eating and laughing. When it reached her pubic bone and bit down hard, she was finally able to scream.

Chimalis bolted upright in bed, sweat beading on her skin, her chest heaving with rapid, uncontrollable breaths. It was dark, save for a sliver of Aspen sunlight speared across her bed.

Her alarm clock blared; 6:30 AM. She groaned, grabbed the clock in both hands, and tossed it across the room.

"Damn!" she said, slamming her fist onto her nightstand. "Another freaking nightmare."

And of the same creature, that terrible Atasaya, the Zuni monster that she had vanquished less than a month ago. Why? Why this creature? There had been so many others over the years. A Dzoavits who feasted on children at a K-12 magnet school in Sandpoint, Idaho. That Kigatilik in Canada killing off Inuit shaman. And let's not forget those Mapuche demons causing all sorts of mischief in South-Central Chile. Snuffing those creatures out had taken an international effort and the death of Chimalis' fiancée, who sacrificed himself for the group. Why, then, was the Atasaya rising so prominently in her dreams?

The reason why would have to wait. It was early, the sun had risen, she was running late, and there was a lot of paperwork waiting on her office desk.

She rubbed sleep from her eyes, yawned, stretched, and tried to put the matter out of her mind.

She drank some water, took a pee, did her thirty minutes of yoga, then showered. The warm water felt good against her skin, and so she paused, closed her eyes, and finally had a moment of good thoughts.

Her vacation was coming up. She had not put in for it yet, but she intended to—today, for sure. A warm, sandy beach in California—Malibu, Santa Monica, Laguna—or perhaps this year she'd hit the Rockies for a little hiking, or New York for some bar-hopping with a hook-up or two. She had options. The key was to go somewhere free of all the nasties of the world, those little paranormal darlings that plagued persons like her 24/7. The Bureau had a database and digital chart indicating the current hotspots of paranormal activity across the Americas. She needed to log in today, find the quietest location, and then put in her request. Today… it had to be today.

She was three bites into her toast and guacamole spread when her cell phone erupted. She ignored it. It rang again and again. On the fourth ring, she answered, knowing exactly who it was, but pretending she didn't, just to tick him off. "Chimalis Burton, FBI. May I help you?"

"Hola, Chimalis. Como estas esta manana?"

Her partner, Luiz Vasquez, was a noob with the Bureau. In the field only two years, his pleasant attitude in the mornings was cause for outrage, though she did appreciate his positive attitude on life. Chimalis wished she shared it more often.

"I'm eating my breakfast, Louie," she said, greeting him informally while talking through her chewing. "Can't this wait until I get to the office?"

She could feel him shaking his head on the other side. "I'm afraid not. Beaucoup baddie activity in Laredo. The chief wants us on a plane by eleven. I'm securing tickets right now."

"Laredo's more Joe Littlecloud's territory," she said with a big sigh. "Can't they pull him in?"

"*Nada*. They got him in Memphis dealing with some kind of Chickasaw demon. Some long, black shadow-like thing terrorizing a lawyer."

A *Nalusa Falaya*. She knew the creature well but had so far been fortunate not to have dealt with one. "Bernard, then. A little out of his discipline, but he's qualified."

"They want us, Chimalis." A pause, then, "They want *you*."

Of course. *A dozen other agents were more than qualified to deal with whatever it was on the border, and they send my ass in all the way from Colorado.* She rolled her eyes. *Smart!*

"Fine." Chimalis checked the time. "I'll meet you at DIA by nine, ten at the latest. You have a briefing of what this is all about, I assume?"

"Oh, yes," Luiz said, his accent thick. "And it's a doozy!"

Chimalis doubted that. Except for her nightmare and those other assignments she had remembered upon waking, most cases that she was given turned out to be nothing. False alarms or minor matters best left to priests or local astrologers. She did not like the idea of heading to the border, and on such short notice. She hated the border, in fact. She hated the notion of a barrier between peoples, and she most certainly didn't like being there amidst all the political and human hardship and not having the authority to do anything about it. She was an FBI agent, true, but her authority was quite limited in that capacity.

She finished her breakfast, brushed her teeth and hair, dashed on a little perfume, and put on a simple cord of beads. She packed lightly, assuming her visit to Laredo would be short. When she got there, she'd figure out a way to pass the investigation to an agent in that jurisdiction and be back in Aspen by midnight.

As Chimalis opened the door to leave, she paused in front of the hearth of her electric fireplace and stared at the Zuni ritual knife resting on the mantel. Sheathed comfortably in the leather holster given to her by her mother. She eyed the hilt and its emblazoned symbols of defeated Cryptids, including the symbol of that damnable Atasaya of her nightmare. The symbols were not lit with fire as they often were when the blade vanquished another spirit. They were quiet, cold, non-threatening. Rather lovely in their silent repose, a far cry from the horrifying souls they represented.

Chimalis cursed, then grabbed the blade and tucked it into her purse. This little junket to Laredo might be nothing, but better safe than sorry. She didn't want to take it; it was always a pain to get it through security at the airport, even though she was an FBI agent.

She zipped up her purse, mumbled a short Zuni prayer for strength, and headed out the door.

Chapter Two

The scene at the border was a disgrace, and it angered Chimalis to her bones.

The smell was immediately recognizable: human rot brought on rapidly by incessant heat and humidity. The somber mood of everyone in attendance, speaking low and moving about in their duties, a stilted, zombie-like homage to the dead. And there were dead bodies. Lots and lots of them.

Mexicans and probably Central Americans trying to get over the border, packed into the back of a semi. A border agent somewhere along the line had clearly looked the other way, undoubtedly incentivized by a wad of cash. Their short-lived journey to a better life cut short by —

By what?

Chimalis and Luiz picked through the area cordoned off by yellow tape and a regiment of local police, FBI forensics, border agents, DEA, you name it. The media were positioned in the Joint Information Center about fifty yards away, though that did not seem to faze many of them. They kept breaking through the no-go line to get a peek at the carnage on display.

"Agent Chimalis Burton? I'm Leburn Grace, Laredo Chief of Police."

Chief Grace offered his hand, and Chimalis took it. "Nice to meet you," she said, more perfunctory than sincere. The man had a reasonably pleasant visage and demeanor, though she could tell that years of cigarette smoke had put deep grey lines on his forehead and tarnish on his teeth. He was sweaty and smelled of stress. She couldn't blame him.

"Thank you for allowing us into your jurisdiction," she said, then dared a look up into the back of the truck. This close, she could smell dried blood and a strong residue of human waste. Many of the victims had already been removed, tagged, put in body bags, and laid out in a tidy row alongside the road. "How many victims in total?"

"Twenty-six," he said as he removed his cap to wipe his brow, "including the driver. All dead."

She had gotten a preliminary de-brief from Luiz, which clarified why she had been called in. She now wished she had packed a heavier suitcase. "All from self-inflicted wounds? None from heat and/or suffocation?"

Chief Grace shook his head. "Not unless your people have found something new." He motioned into the truck where a small forensics team worked.

"If I may take a look?" Chimalis asked, pointing into the truck.

"Be my guest," Chief Grace said. "It's your case now."

Luiz took the stepladder first, and then assisted Chimalis into the trailer. They were greeted by the head of the forensics team that the local FBI office had dispatched. No official agent, however, had been assigned yet. They had been waiting for Chimalis to take over.

She slipped on a pair of nitrile gloves and got to work.

What a mess! She kept saying it over and over in her mind, shaking her head, sighing. She'd seen worse over her career, crime scenes that defied logic, defied rational thought and decency. The carnage inflicted by those Mapuche demons in the Andes had given her reasons to retire, not to mention her most recent showdown with that Atasaya. But this... this was strange in a way that she hadn't experienced before.

"Looks like we might have a werewolf on our hands," Luiz said somewhere behind her.

Chimalis nodded. "Maybe." Some of the wounds on the bodies lying before her, all twisted and contorted in death, fit the pattern. There were large claw marks across faces and exposed chests. But as the preliminary report had stated, most of the wounds were self-inflicted, including human bite marks. And it was rare—in fact, almost unheard of—for a lycanthrope to begin feasting before it had fully changed. No. Some of the damage fit the definition of a werewolf attack, but not enough to convince her. Something else had done this. Something with the power to turn an entire trailer of desperate, frightened people into blood-crazed cannibals.

She reached over the cold, stiffening body of a heavy-set man and pulled away a scarf lying over the face of a young girl. Chimalis tugged at the scarf to pull it away from the grasp of a lady whose mutilated and half-eaten face lay on the girl's chest. Probably the mother, she thought, and perhaps the heavy man was the father. What a sweet, terrible tableau. Chimalis ran her fingers through the dry locks of the girl's hair. "I'm so sorry, honey. I'll find out what did this to you. To you *all*."

She pocketed the scarf. Against the rules to remove evidence from a crime scene, but so what? No one was looking at her, and besides, she'd learned long ago that when dealing with the supernatural, such innocuous things like a scarf could, in the end, prove useful. If for no other reason but to serve as a constant reminder that these people, this innocent girl lying in lifeless repose before her, nestled against her mother and father, deserved justice.

"I'm done, Louie," she said, standing and pulling off her gloves. "I'll review the full forensics report once it's available. What do we know about the driver?"

Luiz scribbled a few final notes, tucked away his pad and pencil, then said, "A petty criminal. Undocumented. Forged papers that allowed him to travel back and forth across the border on missions such as this."

"What about *his* wounds?"

"Self-inflicted as well. He apparently stopped the truck and then drew a Bowie across his throat. Deep, too. Right to the bone. Then he just sat there and bled out."

"That doesn't sound like a werewolf attack, does it?"

Luiz smiled and shook his head. "No, it doesn't."

"These people were coerced, Louie, manipulated into killing themselves and then made to feast upon their kills. Whatever caused it, fed as well, but only after the fact. Is that courtesy, you figure? Does it consider that kind of restraint honest, perhaps even noble?"

Luiz considered. "Perhaps, though I've never been able to get into the mind of a supernatural creature the way you do."

Few people could. Unfortunately, she had a special gift that the Bureau didn't hesitate to utilize in such situations. The hands-down best, however, was Joe Littlecloud. As an Apache *di-yin*, a shaman, he had an inherent connection with the spirits that she envied, and oh how she wished he were here now. Perhaps she'd call upon him for advice if things got difficult... and they would. They always did, and if this was something that could spread madness like a virus, the situation could escalate quickly and become a national crisis. The question was: how far could this creature, or whatever it was, spread the madness? Did it have to be close to its victims, like in the enclosed box of an eighteen-wheeler? Or could it project further, say, fifty yards? One hundred? More? There were more questions now than answers. "I need to speak with the first officer on the scene," Chimalis said, walking to the end of the truck. Chief Grace helped her down. "I need to know what he found, and—"

She saw Luiz's and Chief Grace's uncomfortable expressions. "What?"

Luiz shot a glance at the chief, then said, "Officer Torres has just been hospitalized and is currently under sedation, Chimalis. He's lost his mind, like all these poor folk."

NEAR STONEMAN LAKE, ARIZONA

Golden Eyes felt a tickle of fear. The sensation ran along the grey fur of his back, through his shoulders, and ended at the top of his long, wolf-like ears. It was not the kind of fear that he felt all the time: from other Alpha males threatening to steal his pack or from poachers or farmers violating hunting laws. He could live with that kind of fear, for he had ways of turning those creatures/humans away and driving them mad if necessary. This was a fear that he hadn't felt in almost three decades. Not since he had crossed the border and settled in the United States, in Arizona. This kind of fear meant only one thing.

Isai. Red Eyes has found me.

It felt strange hearing his brother's name in his mind. It had been years since Golden Eyes had thought of him. He hadn't thought of his human name in a long time either: *Miguel.* It felt strange hearing that one, too, like a kind of blasphemy against all that was holy. Golden Eyes and his brother were no more human now than the moment they had been turned by that angry magician all those many years ago. God had forsaken them on that day due to his brother's—his own—disrespect for the old man, and since that day, they had been cursed to roam forever through El Salvador, Guatemala, Belize, Costa Rica, Panama, Nicaragua, on up into Mexico, and now, the United States. Golden Eyes thought he had finally escaped his brother's influence and grasp. He was wrong.

Isai is coming.

But he was still far away. His presence felt like the faint scent of rot or sickness that oftentimes blew through the woods outside a farmer's ranch, just before Golden Eyes and the pack went hunting for meat. It was like the faint scent of human sweat and testosterone that he smelled when poachers were near. The sensation, the fear, was faint but closing. Isai was seeking Miguel's scent, his aura, and he would, in time, find it. It was all a matter of time.

I must leave here. I must leave to save the pack.

That's what Golden Eye's instinct told him. When in the midst of real danger, flee, run, and make sure the pack was safe.

There were fifteen wolves total in his pack, which was rather large. It was more like two packs combined, the result of an older Alpha dying and Golden Eyes showing mercy and allowing its widowed mate and kin to come and be a part of his group. Four mated pairs of eight, the rest cubs and young adults. Golden Eyes himself was not mated with any, though some of the females had tried to breed with him over the years. He couldn't. Not that he was physically incapable. He held the same desires and instincts that any other wolf in the pack held. But he would not breed with any of them, for what kind of cubs could he produce? Ones with hooves instead of claws? Ones with tiny horns peeking out of their malformed skulls? No. He would not condemn any cub, any child, to the same curse and fate that he had brought upon himself. And why had he brought all this upon himself? Because he had not been strong enough to stop Red Eyes from stealing that magician's food, from breaking the agreement that they had made with the old man to fetch firewood for his fireplace. Because he, Miguel, was never strong enough to fight back.

Not anymore…

Golden Eyes rose from the warm slab of rock on which he rested and returned to the pack. Some were sleeping. Some chewing on the remains of a small deer that they had killed just that morning. Cubs were playing. A breeding pair was breeding again, and despite many decades of walking and living among them, Golden Eyes still felt uncomfortable in the presence of such carnal activities. The residual feeling of being human, being Christian, of having shame. And perhaps that was the most terrible part of the curse: remembering, even in small parts, what it was like to be human. To have human desires and yet, be incapable of acting on those desires, those needs. Isai had rebelled against his condemnation in the most despicable ways. And Golden Eyes had never been strong enough to stop him.

He raised his large, powerful muzzle and howled. It was more a howl and guttural whistle combined, for he was not entirely wolfen. He howled/whistled again and again, and finally, the pack roused itself from its activities and gathered round.

He projected his thoughts, his emotions, into each of their minds, telling them goodbye and giving them direction as to how to move forward without him. He told them he was dying and that he was leaving to find a place of peace to bring on the final repose. It was a lie, at least in part. He was not dying today, or tomorrow, or the next day, but he *was* heading toward death, wasn't he? Somewhere out there, in Arizona, or New Mexico, or maybe even Texas, death awaited him, but he could not bring himself to tell them of his brother, for they would, instinctively, want to come along and protect him, for he was their leader, their pack-mate. *Defend the pack!* But he could not, would not, lead them to their deaths. He had to leave. He had to go alone. He had to face death by himself, and this time, he would *not* turn away.

Golden Eyes touched his muzzle to each of theirs in turn. He nipped at the belly of a cub who seemed saddened by his departure. He made it clear by his actions which male he wanted to lead the pack in his absence. He licked each muzzle and spent time grooming their necks. Then he howled once more and held it until the rest howled with him, in one long, beautiful symphony that raised his spirits and gave him courage. *They will be all right*, he thought. *They will go on without me… and thrive.*

He turned and clopped away. He did not know exactly where he was going or how far he would have to travel. Out there somewhere was his brother, Isai, who called himself Red Eyes, and Golden Eyes would find him by letting his fear, his hope, lead the way.

Chapter Three

Officer Torres was, as her late father would have put it, as mad as a hatter. In a padded cell and a straitjacket, for it had been deemed that he was a threat to himself and others.

Chimalis observed him for thirty minutes from behind a two-way glass. Just watching, listening, trying to hear anything that might give her some clue as to what he had experienced at the crime scene. She had learned long ago in situations like this that a witness (or a victim, in this case) would sometimes confess to themselves the truth of the horror they had seen. Officer Torres constantly mumbled in Spanish. Chimalis was reasonably competent in the language, but he spoke too low, and sometimes, he just mouthed the words.

"I want to speak with him alone," she said to the attending physician at the Laredo Border Hospital for Mental Health. "Alone, no guards."

"I don't think that's wise, Agent Burton," the man said, clearly surprised that she had even suggested it. "He's just arrived. He's tanked up on sedatives. He needs a little time to—"

"No, now." She was already growing impatient. "I need to speak to him while the situation is fresh in his mind, however much mind he has left. You can post a guard outside the door if you like. He's in a jacket. He's sedated. I'll be fine."

"You want to go in there?"

She nodded. "Yes."

The man scratched his chin. "We could move him to another room with a table, put him in chains, and lock them down so that he cannot attack you. It would only take ten minutes to secure."

"No." She pointed to the glass. "In there. Right now."

The man paused, then said, "Okay. You're the boss. But I want it on the record that this is against my objection. I cannot guarantee your safety. Without further restraints, he might attack. You understand that?"

I hope he does. "I understand."

As they let her in, she advised Luiz to take strict notes while monitoring their encounter through the glass. They would have access to the camera footage afterward, of course, but notes were necessary and much easier to refer to once they were in the field conducting their investigation. The key here, however, was to figure out what they were looking for. Only Officer Javier Torres knew the answer, whether he realized it or not.

The room smelled of human funk. *Perhaps he soiled himself,* Chimalis thought as she moved carefully into the room, with no protection, no weapon, nothing to keep this disturbed, agitated man from striking.

Torres had been stripped of his uniform and was now in common grey sweats and shirt, though one could barely see the shirt due to the straitjacket. His dark hair was a rat's nest; his face, a forest of black stubble.

"Hello, Officer Javier Torres. I am Agent Chimalis Burton, FBI-VPA. I would like to speak to you about the eighteen-wheeled Peterbilt you found last night with twenty-six corpses."

Torres shook his head as if he'd awakened from sleep. He looked up at her from the corner he had crawled into. "FBI-VPA?"

"The Federal Bureau of Investigations, Violent Paranormal Activities Division."

He nodded, then, "Twenty-six? All of them?"

"All of them, including the driver. Can we speak about that?"

Torres pushed himself up the wall with his legs. He groaned as if every move was painful. Chimalis heard his knees crack as he pushed. "Twenty-six?"

"Yes. All brutally murdered by their own hands, which is odd, don't you think, Officer Torres? Normally, when you find a situation like this on the Texas border, the occupants—almost always Mexicans or Central Americans—die from suffocation, heat exhaustion, dehydration. They don't stab their children, their brothers, sisters. They don't bash their heads in and then feast on the remains. Do you agree with my assessment?"

Torres shook his head erratically. He moved from the corner but clung to the wall, sliding along as if he were attached to it with Velcro. Chimalis found the sound that the straitjacket made eerily soothing as it scrapped against the lightly padded wall. Like an ASMR video of a young lady, or man, whispering to put you to sleep, but in some dark context for adult roleplaying. "Oh yes, yes. Very odd. Very, very odd."

"How do you account for those deaths, Officer Torres? What did you see last night? Your report—what little the officers that responded to your call for aid could determine—stated that you saw a goat. A goat, Officer Torres? Why did you lie to them?"

He shook his head vigorously, droplets of spit flying from his quivering chin. "Yes, yes, it was a goat... no, not a goat, not exactly. It was a wolf... no, that's not right, either."

Chimalis dared to draw closer. She leaned in closer and looked him straight in the eye. "What was it? What did you see? What came out of that truck? You mumbled to the responding officers that something knocked you down, and that's why you lost your bolt cutters. What was it? What knocked you down?"

Torres' breathing grew more erratic, his breath foul. He looked at her with red and watery eyes. Chimalis was almost close enough to see herself in his eyes, if not for his constant blinking. She was hoping to see something else, for it was often the case that a person possessed by a malevolent spirit flashed the beast through the eyes. No such luck here. The only thing haunting Officer Torres's eyes was memory.

"It spoke to me through the box," Torres said with tiny gasps of air. "It told me to open the door and come see. I—I couldn't refuse. It was like an overwhelming pleasure, you know, like it had not actually ordered me to do it, like it was my idea from the beginning. I *wanted* to open that door. *Entiende?*"

Chimalis nodded and pulled away a step to give him breathing room. "Yes, I understand. Please, go on."

He paused to catch his breath, then, "I cut the chain, you see. Cut it right in two. Then opened the door… and it attacked me. It hit me square in the chest. I fell back. I reached for my bolt cutters, but they had scattered away. I then tried to draw my *pistola*, but it put its hoof on my hand to prevent me from—"

"Its hoof?"

"Yes, its hoof. It had hooves, just like a goat, like I said. It put its hoof on my hand to keep me from drawing my gun, and it looked at me, sizing me up, you know, like it was trying to figure out if I was worthy of its teeth."

"Then it *was* a wolf?"

Torres shook his head, more spit and sweat spraying outward. "No, not entirely. It had tiny little horns peeking out of its head, like little buds you might see on a young deer just before you blast it with a rifle. I could tell because of the light from my patrol car. Teeth like a wolf, horns and hooves like a goat. I told this to my fellow officers, to that waste of space doctor here, but they just thought I was crazy. But I'm not crazy. You hear me. Not crazy!"

Chimalis moved back another pace, waiting for him to try something, but he didn't. He calmed, mumbled again in Spanish, and then continued. "Its eyes were blood red. No, no, no, no… not like mine. Not bloodshot. But red. Deep red. And they glowed when it spoke."

"It could talk?"

"No. Not like you and me. Through the *mente*… the mind. It told me to turn away, to look away, or I would die."

"And did you look away?"

Torres nodded. "Yes. Otherwise, I would have died, wouldn't I? I tried not to. I tried keeping its gaze, but I turned away like it ordered me to."

"Then what happened?" Chimalis asked, feeling like she was on the edge of her seat in a movie theater, popcorn in hand, waiting with bated breath for that final reveal that all good action and suspense pictures made.

"Nothing. Nothing. It just walked away, slow and steady, like it had all the time in the world. It clopped along like a goat walking across the road."

"And then you went mad."

"I'm not mad! I saw what I saw. It was real. It was—"

"I've just spoken with Captain Williams. You're being brought up on charges for murder." Chimalis hated to lie to the poor man, but it was necessary.

"Wait! Why? I did nothing wrong. I killed no one."

Chimalis shrugged. "All twenty-six of those people died because of your inaction. You did not kill whatever it was you saw. You let it go, and therefore, you're an accessory to murder."

He grew more erratic, wilder as he paced back and forth along the wall. "No, no. I followed procedure. I called for backup. I tried to save those people. It wasn't my fault."

"It was," she said, matching his pacing, shadowing his moves so that she was always in front of him. "Captain Williams says that at least half of those people could have survived had you acted faster, cut that chain quicker."

"*Cadena, cadena, cadena…*"

"What is that you're whispering? What are you saying?"

"No, it isn't my fault. Not my fault!"

"Then whose fault was it, Officer Torres? Whose?"

He leapt at her. He launched like a missile, his arms still locked in the straitjacket. She was thankful for that, for he head-butted her like the goat he described, knocking her down and then trying to get at her throat with gnashing, biting teeth. He was big, strong, and even in his incapacitated state, she found it difficult to fight him off. He spat in her face, screaming a name over and over. In the danger of the moment, Chimalis could not tell exactly what the name was, but she committed his gibberish to memory.

Security burst in and pulled Torres away. Chimalis reached for her throat to ensure he hadn't bitten her. Luckily, no cuts, though it did feel sore where he had tried to gnaw her skin.

Luiz came in and pulled her out of the room. When they were safely in the hall, and the door to Officer Torres's padded cell closed, he said, "That was foolish, boss. He could have hurt you badly."

Chimalis rubbed her neck and gave her heart rate time to slow. "Yes, but he didn't, and it was a necessary risk to get what we needed."

Luiz shook his head. "And what was that?"

Chimalis grabbed the notepad in his hand. She scanned it quickly, marked a line with her finger, recalled what she had committed to memory from the encounter, and turned the pad around to show him. She smiled and winked. "A name."

SAN ANTONIO, TEXAS

The journey had been long, unforgiving, but Red Eyes had made it. He'd crossed the border and was now on the hunt. That's how he imagined his situation. He was hunting for Golden Eyes, for Miguel, his brother. Red Eyes could feel him now, faintly, and as long as there was a whiff of Miguel's presence, even a vague tickle on the edge of his consciousness, he'd keep hunting.

Where to go next was the question. The United States was big. He had heard villagers in El Salvador, Guatemala, and Honduras speak of a land that stretched far into a frozen forest near the very top of the earth. Red Eyes knew that Miguel couldn't have wandered that far; he was never one for cold weather. Miguel was near. Red Eyes could feel him. But where exactly?

The big city of San Antonio seemed the most logical place to start. It also gave Red Eyes feasting opportunities, and he'd need his strength to confront Miguel.

My brother. Red Eyes barked-snorted the words as if it amounted to nothing but a smear of phlegm, something to discard in the gutter or in the piles of waste in the dumpster that he currently sat beside in a dark alley near a busy thoroughfare. *My sweet brother, Miguel. For thirty years, you've been blaming me for Sumpul River, for El Mozote, for El Calabozo. But they were not my fault...*

Not my fault!

And Miguel would now finally pay for leaving him behind, abandoning Red Eyes to the privations of the peasants for all those years. It had taken him thirty years to find Golden Eyes. Perhaps he should have known that his brother would flee north. *Coward!*

He'd eaten little since escaping that truck in Laredo. Oh, but that was choice meat, fresh, warm, and plentiful. Had the air not been so hot, so stagnant in the back of that sweltering metal box, he might have stayed longer. If he'd had enough time, he might have grabbed hold of one of the younger ones and dragged it off into the desert for later consumption, but his plans had been thwarted by that Good Samaritan, that so-called Officer Torres who had come poking around. Humans like that always did, which was why Red Eyes had avoided crossing the border for so long: too many chances to be discovered. Too many chances to be caught and killed.

Can I be killed? It was a question he had asked himself many times since that first moment after the magician's curse. Many a person had tried over the years to settle the answer, especially during the El Salvadoran civil war. Those attempts had been thwarted, and those people had suffered. Red Eyes didn't know whether he could be killed or not. It didn't matter right now, anyway. His immediate concern was finding his brother, and then death, if it came, would not matter.

"Come on out, fella," a voice said to Red Eyes from the artificial white light of the street. A silhouette stood in front of him at the mouth of the alley, large, brooding, anxious, but easily recognizable. Another one of those self-proclaimed Good Samaritans. "Come on out, or I'll have to arrest you."

The man had a pistol in his hand. He held it forward, lazily, as if he didn't expect a serious confrontation. Red Eyes moved closer. He had no intention of killing this man or killing anyone. That was not his style, unless it was absolutely necessary. At the moment, it was not. He'd let this man, this officer of the law, do the killing for him.

Red Eyes did as he was ordered. He moved out of the darkness of the alley and into the light.

The officer backed away a pace, surprised by the appearance of a dog. He kept his pistol trained forward. "You're not a person. You're a wol—a wolf—what the hell are you?"

What indeed? I am your liberator, your salvation. I will give you peace, rest from all your troubles. And they are myriad, aren't they, Officer Collins? Your wife and the neighbor who always seems to be around. The debt that keeps piling up. Your son failing school. Your mother on life support. And all of them expecting you to solve their problems. Such a burden to bear, plus being responsible for the safety and security of all the people in these bars and restaurants that care nothing for you. They laugh at you. They ignore your existence. So, let me free you from those burdens and their ridicule. Turn from me… turn, and I will show you peace.

Red Eyes moved even closer and flashed his pulsing red eyes wide. Officer Collins turned as ordered. He turned, lowered his gun, and stared at his salvation.

A bar. A hole in the wall. Neon sign flashing 'Open.' Booming music. Laughter. *Go*, Red Eyes said through Officer Collins' confused mind. *Go and find your salvation. I give you leave to do so.*

The man nodded and walked across the street.

The bouncer at the door was the first person Officer Collins shot. Three bullets in the chest. He stepped over the body and pushed the door open. A moment's pause, then more shots. Over and over and over. *Boomboomboom!* Then screaming, running. People trying to get out. Confused patrons on the sidewalks outside paused to see what was going on and then ran themselves. *Boomboomboom!* And then, a long, long pause. A final pause, and then a final shot.

If Red Eyes could smile, he'd do so. Instead, he shook the dust of the road off his fur, licked drool from his thin, dark lips, and trotted across the road. In the confusion of the moment, no one noticed a stray dog entering the bar. No one even seemed to care as they scattered for their own lives.

The bar was a mess. Bodies and blood everywhere. Men and women both. No children this time, which was good, Red Eyes supposed. Their flesh was tender, true, but he grew weary of killing the innocent. He preferred killing adults. Well, not killing them in the classic sense; more like encouraging them to give in to the urges they'd had all their lives: express their rage freely over one problem or another weighing heavily on their shoulders. *I am a liberator*, he thought, feeling good about himself. *Like God, I am salvation.*

Red Eyes' stomach growled. He found Officer Collins on the floor alongside the casing of that last bullet he shot through the roof of his own mouth. Red Eyes yipped his joy. Nice, choice meat awaited.

Red Eyes paused. He wanted to bite into the officer's neck, but no, not this time. No need to draw attention to this. Let this look like a domestic terror attack. Drink instead.

He lapped Officer Collins' blood off the floor, where it pooled around the man's shattered head. It was warm, sweet, salty, and just what Red Eyes needed. A few bits of brain matter found their way onto his tongue. He'd take it. Tomorrow, he'd find other meat to consume. For now, he'd be content with just a savory cocktail. It was a bar, after all.

Sirens blared outside, drawing closer. Red Eyes finished the last spot of blood near Officer Collins' head. He licked his lips, looked left, then right to ensure a safe exit. There was no one near to stop him.

He fled out the back. The door to the alley had been nearly ripped off by those trying to escape the slaughter. Red Eyes slipped into the shadows easily and trotted away as if he were taking a slow, pleasant stroll through a garden.

Tomorrow, he'd find more food. And tomorrow, he'd continue to move toward the scent of his brother that grew stronger and stronger in his mind every minute.

Chapter Four

What the hell are we dealing with here? Chimalis wondered as she surveyed the evidence on the bar floor. The bodies of the mass shooting in the bar had already been removed. Six people had been gunned down by an off-duty officer moonlighting as a security guard who walked into the bar and started firing. Thirty wounded. Eyewitnesses at the scene said the man had a confused, deranged look as if he didn't know what he was doing. Then he put the gun in his own mouth and pulled the trigger. Local police and non-VPA FBI agents were investigating it as a domestic terrorist attack or just some crackpot who snapped, though nothing in Officer Collins' background, or on his social media pages, on his phone, or in his apartment, suggested any affiliation with terrorist or neo-Nazi or anarchist groups, nor did it seem that he was connected with any foreign terrorist organization. He was a plain-Jane, normal American police officer who, for some inexplicable reason, decided to walk into a bar and start shooting. Such things had happened in the past, Chimalis knew, but this one didn't add up.

Canvassing after forensics had had their sweep of the place was not the most ideal way to investigate a potential VPA crime scene. Too much evidence had already been removed. The fact that she couldn't study the bodies herself was a problem as well. She and Luiz had stopped by the local coroner's office to look at them, but by then, it was too late. She needed to see them where they had fallen, the spatter of blood, the confused angle of broken limbs, the dishevelment of the entire locale. All that remained on the scene now was yellow caution tape and small notes and markings to indicate where the bodies had fallen. That wasn't good enough in her experience, but what could she do? The local authorities were not treating this mass casualty event as VPA. Chimalis had come here on her own after Luiz had scoured the FBI database for recent crimes with possible links to the Laredo massacre. She'd come here against the recommendations of her superiors, who thought her investigation would be best served closer to the initial contact with whatever it was that had perpetrated the Laredo tragedy. But Chimalis had a hunch that whatever caused the Laredo disaster had caused this one as well. And whatever did this was on the move.

She knelt and studied the spot where the shooter had taken his life. She ran her fingers across the hardwood floor where the officer had lain to see if she could divine any life force, any supernatural presence. Even if this tragic event had nothing to do with her investigation, it did not mean that there weren't spiritual baddies involved. She sensed nothing. Just a cold, hardwood floor. Just a spot in a bar where a seemingly normal guy killed many innocents and then blew his own brains out.

There were three things odd about this crime scene. First, none of the bodies had been eaten. Forensics found no evidence of bite marks pre- or post-mortem. That suggested that this event had nothing to do with her case. On the other hand, the shooter had placed a pistol in his mouth and pulled the trigger. The bullet ripped through the back of his head with a hefty spray of blood and brain matter. Problem was, there was very little blood found pooled beside the body, nor did they find much brain matter afterward.

There were some pistol models where the concussive power and energy expelled by firing could partially incinerate brain tissue, but Officer Collins used a standard-issue Smith & Wesson M&P9. A decent firearm, but incapable of such force. So, where were the man's blood and brains? The forensics officer jacked up on strong coffee commented to Chimalis, with a chuckle, that you had to be brainless to commit such a terrible crime. True enough, she admitted, but the reason for lack of brain tissue was clear to her: the creature, the entity they were searching for, had consumed it all.

Luiz came out of the stockroom and knelt beside Chimalis. "Are you picking up any energies, boss?"

Chimalis shook her head. "Nope. It's clean." She stood with a deep sigh. "I can't prove that this is the result of our perp, but I just know it is. It feels like it is. I don't know if I can get our boss to buy it, though."

"You won't have to prove purchase," he said, motioning her to follow. "Let me show you what I found."

He guided her behind the bar and into the stockroom. The door to the back alley was open. Warm sunlight filtered into the room. Nothing unusual or out of place here. The police report had said that a few of the walking wounded had escaped through the back door, but they had reported seeing nothing out of the ordinary in the alley. Chimalis had hoped that perhaps one of the eyewitnesses would have remembered seeing something in their escape. Nothing. Which meant one of two things: they weren't paying attention to the details because they were fleeing for their lives, or that this creature, perhaps, had the power of illusion. The first option was the most likely, but Chimalis had learned long ago that when dealing with VPA, the second option was just as viable. In paranormal work, sometimes the simplest answer was not always the right one.

Sorry, Sherlock.

Luiz led her into the alley. Nothing odd about it. Standard alley with empty boxes and wooden pallets stacked up alongside a green trash bin. Discarded bits of paper and beer labels strewn across the dirty pavement. A distinct smell of stale alcohol and sweat. Urine as well.

"What are you showing me, Louie?" Chimalis asked.

He cleared his throat. "Well, I figured that since local PD are treating this as a non-VPA event, that they would overlook details that we might consider important. Since they had the perp dead on the floor, why bother spending a lot of time in the alley, am I right?"

Chimalis nodded. "You often are."

"*Gracias,*" he said with a small bow and a smile. "So I rummaged around." He led her to the trash bin and kicked aside a wet cardboard box. "I found these."

Praise Jesus! She wasn't Christian, but it never hurt to thank a higher power at a time like this. She pulled out her cell and took several pictures, pictures of two perfectly formed prints of bloody hoof marks. Faint, easily missed as nothing but dirt and/or paint, but she recognized them right away.

She tucked away her phone, her adrenaline rising. "Well, we know one thing about our little baddy: it's smart, very brutal, but it ain't no genius.

"Seems like it causes and then feeds on human misery. It creates these terrible moments of violence to then have ample food sources. But it knows it's being hunted and is in danger. Thus, it tries to hide its involvement by drinking only the blood and eating existing brain matter, which can be easily overlooked or discarded as unimportant. And yet, it pauses here, for whatever reason, and leaves its mark. Stupid."

"Or," Luiz suggested, being delicate not to offend, "it wants us to find it."

Chimalis nodded. Some supernatural forces were painfully arrogant and self-destructive. That Atasaya that she had tracked down in Colorado was a primary example of the weakness of the breed. Chimalis was happy about that kind of arrogance, the type of self-absorption that was oftentimes the only way humans could get close enough to defeat the bastards. Either this creature was sloppy or, as Luiz said, it wanted to be found.

"In either case," Chimalis said, "we know it's been here, it has hooves, and it's on the move."

She paused, looked around, then said, "Where is it going? That's the question. Texas is a big state. From here, it can go in many directions. If it's moving by the main highway, it can take

I-10 east to Houston or head west to Kerrville, Sonora, all the way to El Paso. If I-35, Austin and Dallas."

"A hoofed creature can't travel very far," Luiz said. "At least not without taking serious breaks to rest. We could catch up."

Chimalis nodded. "But I suspect it isn't moving by hoof alone. Just consider the distance between here and the border. It's hitching rides somehow, and if so, it could be anywhere in a very short amount of time. So, where is it going?"

There was a pause in their discussion as she continued searching the alley, hoping to find a spot of decayed brain matter or anything else that would give further clues as to the nature of this creature that was keeping one, two steps ahead of them. That needed to change, Chimalis knew. They would never find the creature if they were always playing catch-up.

"Okay," she said, turning to Luiz, "time to do some significant research on this matter. I need to try to discover the physical and spiritual nature of this thing. Without more information, we're working in the blind. I'll be returning to Aspen tonight.

"Run the data we have through the VPA's central computer to give us options as to the most likely direction a creature like this might move. I suspect north or northwest. Leaving Laredo, it could have moved in any direction. It chose San Antonio, and I suspect it's pretty bullheaded when it picks a route. But let's see. Give us options, and then we'll decide where to move next, and maybe we can get a jump on it.

"Then, hop a plane to Corpus Christi and get Father de Seña's holy backside here in two days. We'll all meet up again here to make our next move. I don't know what the hell we're dealing with yet, Luis, but whatever it is, I want all the firepower we can get."

ASPEN, COLORADO

Catching a last-minute flight from San Antonio to Aspen was not Chimalis's idea of a pleasant trip. Not an overly long flight, thankfully, but time was relative when going through brutal wind shear and rain pockets. Luckily, she had made it back in one piece, she was home, and now she could kick off her shoes, relax, and do some quality research. For a short while, at least.

Chimalis loved everything about Aspen: the mountains, the view, the weather, the elevation, the people. Everything. Which was why she had never moved to Denver to be closer to work. She just couldn't bring herself to move away from her childhood home. It had everything she needed, professionally and personally. Most importantly, it possessed one of the largest libraries for paranormal and Cryptid research anywhere in the country, perhaps the world. Her late father's library, and one that he had established over three decades of service as an MI6 agent for the British Secret Intelligence Service.

She took thirty minutes for herself. She checked messages, mail, grabbed a bite to eat. She sat on her sofa with a glass of red wine and thumbed through her cell phone. Luiz had made it to Corpus Christi and was already expressing wonder — or was it shock? — at the number of crosses Father de Seña displayed on his walls. "What do you expect from a retired priest?" she mumbled to herself while giving the young lad the requisite "K" response via text message. Then she pocketed her phone and laid her head back for a ten-minute power nap that turned into twenty.

When she awoke, Chimalis cleared her eyes and focused on the entrance to the library. She yawned, cleared her head, stretched, and then walked through.

A marvelous room. A room dedicated to books upon books upon books from China, Tibet, Africa, South America, Hungary, Russia, and on and on and on. Books too about Native American cultures and mythology, about Cryptid creatures spanning the globe (and the imagination) of every conceivable culture that had risen and fallen from the time of the crusades. Some volumes went back further than that, most of them completely foreign and intellectually unobtainable to Chimalis. She knew English, Spanish, some Portuguese, her own native Zuni, and other Pueblo languages, but not much of anything else, and certainly not

Greek and Latin, which many of the books were in, though some translations had been attempted. Her father had penciled in ample notes along the margins in many of the more intellectually challenging volumes.

Chimalis stood in the center of the library, near the research table, and looked around the room as if it was the first time she had ever been here. She always felt that way when stepping in after a modest absence. The smells of the old but rich leather bindings; the various-sized books squeezed into every spare inch of shelf space; the bright and dark colors of cracked spines with arcane titles over even more arcane names of foreign and very deceased authors. She always gave it all a pause and a modicum of respect before searching.

And then there was Mom and Dad's portrait in a tarnished silver picture frame, sitting as it always did, on the table amidst piles of magazines, old scrolls, and crumpled post-it notes. Her parents, on assignment in Caracas. Young, vibrant, when the world, as they say, was their oyster. Looking at the picture always made Chimalis think of how they met.

In the early 1970s, during the Nixon Administration, Father had been on special assignment for the British government near El Morro, New Mexico, hunting for three British witches who had secretly immigrated to America and who had contorted their bodies into murderous skin-walkers to terrorize the native populations on the nearby Ramah Navajo reservation. Mother, a woman from the Zuni Reservation nearby, was then a rookie for the FBI. She was serving as Dad's liaison to the Bureau. They fell in love. One thing led to another, and *voila*, Chimalis was born fifteen years later.

She had always been surprised that they had waited so long to have a child. At thirteen, Chimalis had asked her father once if she had been an "accident." Her father simply smiled, winked, and said, "No, sweety-peety. You're our greatest legacy." Chimalis had smiled back, hugged him, and accepted his compliment. But Chimalis knew the truth. Their greatest legacy was the library.

Her father had possessed an encyclopedic knowledge of where every book was located on each shelf. Chimalis did not possess such knowledge, so she walked along the back wall, running her fingers over the course, cracked leather, hoping that what she needed would be at arm's length. She was looking for the section dedicated to South and Central American mythology. For that was where she needed to start. The creature that had feasted on the bodies of those poor immigrants, the one that had turned Officer Torres mad, surely had come out of Mexico, Central America, or perhaps even South America. No guarantee of that, of course, since supernatural creatures often liked to roam the globe freely, but it was the best place to start.

After searching for several minutes, she found the South and Central American Cryptids books on the top shelf. Chimalis sighed and shook her head. "Of course they are," she mumbled to herself. "Nothing is ever easy in this business."

She pulled the step ladder over and crawled up until her feet were on the top rung and her face was level with the musty, dusty books dedicated to Cryptid legends from Mexico to Cape Horn. There weren't many, praise Jesus, just a dozen or so, so their review would be relatively easy compared to other parts of the world.

The past few years of service for the Bureau had confined her mostly to investigating Native American Cryptids, like the Atasaya, California Dark-Watchers, or the Ohio Grassman. This apparently hooved creature she was pursuing *could* be American, but what was it really, and did her father have scholarship to identify it?

She ran her hands over the leather bindings of the books to clear away the dust. She always enjoyed leafing through them, especially as a teenager when her father was away on assignment somewhere exotic and her mother was in Denver or Santa Fe or somewhere searching for baddies in the coniferous forests of the Northwest. She had always imagined herself with them, traipsing along on their hikes, their undercover work. They never spoke much about their assignments when alive, but Chimalis could imagine the details, especially through the filter of her own experience. She understood now why Mom and Dad had kept so much to themselves. The particulars would have been unsettling at best, terrifying at worst. Her father's library, however, offered vital knowledge to her now in her assignments.

She picked the three most prominent books on American Cryptids from the shelf and spread them out on the research table. She studied one legend, then another, and another, cross-referencing details and scribbling notes on single-sheet college-ruled paper. There were references to wolf-like creatures; references to goat-like creatures. She read entries for creatures that most likely had nothing whatsoever to do with the one she was after, but she had learned long ago that disconfirming information was just as valuable as confirming. "Eliminate everything that your cryptid is not, Chimalis," her father used to say near the end of his life when it was clear that she was going to follow in her parents' footsteps, "and you will find what you are looking for."

It was clear that her supernatural baddie was not winged, nor was it any type of *chupacabra*, or feline, or reptile. It was most likely canine in nature, judging from some of the bite marks found on the bodies in the Laredo truck. Perhaps a wolf with hooves and little horns. Did such a creature exist? Chimalis shrugged. She'd never heard of one.

She turned the page of book three and found an obscure reference to a legend from El Salvador. A story about a late-night greeting between a black Yoruba magician and two mulatto boys seeking food and rest. The story told of how the magician asked the boys for a favor in exchange for his hospitality, and they had agreed to his wishes. But in the light of morning, they reneged on their agreement and ignored the magician's request. The angry magician then placed a curse on them both, turning them into twisted wolves with horns and —

Chimalis turned the page and searched for a conclusion to the story, but some dark liquid had been spilt on the book and had turned the old, faded ink into dry rivers of black and blue. Her father had scribbled the words "chains" and "El Mozote" in the margins in red pen. She had no idea what either meant, but *El Mozote* was certainly Spanish, and Father had spent a goodly amount of time on assignment in South and Central America in the 1980s. But her mind barely focused on his notes right now. One realization dominated her thoughts.

"Damn," Chimalis said loudly, as an uncomfortable chill ran down her spine, "there are two of them."

Her cell phone vibrated in her pocket. She pulled it out. It was Luiz. The phone vibrated again in her hand. She sighed and answered the call in a more aggressive tone than she had intended.

"What is it, Louie? I'm busy."

He paused, obviously sensing her frustration. "I think you should come to Corpus Christi, boss, as soon as possible. Father de Seña's got something you have to see... and hear."

CHAPTER FIVE

Near the Border of Arizona and New Mexico

It had been a long time since he had resorted to playing the wounded animal, but at this moment in his journey, Golden Eyes needed to use all the skills that the curse had granted him. He hated being deceitful, manipulative, but what other choice did he have? New Mexico was vast, open, dry and desolate in many places. He would never arrive in time on hoof. He needed a ride if he was to stop his brother. Golden Eyes was close enough now to sense Isai working through Texas, killing along the way to satiate his anger.

The approaching truck was nothing more than a pair of white headlights in the distance. Golden Eyes clopped alongside the barren highway and waited for it to draw near. Throwing himself into the on-coming path of a massive, screaming metal monster was a serious risk, and he knew that, despite the curse, he could be killed. There was nothing that he had ever heard about or experienced in his long, torturous life to indicate that he couldn't be smashed flat by a semi moving at over sixty miles per hour. He had never put that theory to the test, of course, but he had put himself in danger many, many times. Usually at the behest of Red Eyes.

As he watched the truck draw near and its lights grow larger, El Mozote came to mind, that terrible, terrible day during the El Salvadoran civil war. So many tragic, useless deaths. *Red Eyes blames me, has always done so, but it wasn't my fault. Not my fault at all. I tried to save those people.*

Now he was awash in the truck's headlights. He turned into the blinding white light, heard and saw the driver lay on the horn and try to slow down.

Golden Eyes leapt into the path of the truck, letting his powerful, cursed goat legs propel him in front of the truck's massive grate and engine compartment. It was close, too close for comfort, but he allowed the truck to graze his left hoof, not enough to damage himself, but enough to turn him over and over in the air, like a propeller from a small plane. Around and around, he twirled until he landed heavily and slid to a stop. The strike on pavement hurt the most, his fur and skin tearing and ripping across the blacktop. He let out a howl loud enough for even the driver to hear. The truck slid a good fifty yards before stopping in a black fog of tire smoke.

Silence, save for Golden Eyes' howls that sounded pitiful and near death. He climbed up slowly on his front legs and scooted himself across the blacktop as if trying to walk. He yelped and yelped and 'managed' to rise onto his uninjured hind hoof, the other dragging. He limped along the side of the road for a few yards and then abruptly sat back down as if he couldn't go on. But he hadn't felt this strong or alive in decades. The magician's curse always ensured that it felt good to deceive and manipulate people and make them do things that they would not normally do, like approaching a wounded, desperate, and potentially dangerous wolf on an empty road.

The driver had not been harmed in his abrupt stop. He climbed out of the cab and checked his truck to ensure it wasn't damaged in the skid. He seemed satisfied with that, and then he turned his attention toward Golden Eyes.

Now... see me as a pet...

"You okay, buddy?" The driver asked, moving slowly toward Golden Eyes. "You okay?"

Golden Eyes planted a deception in the man's mind to make himself look like a chocolate lab. He whimpered and howled and lay down on the blacktop, rolling up to expose his belly, a sign of submission and trust.

The driver knelt beside him and touched Golden Eyes' supposed wounded hind leg, which now resembled a Labrador's leg perfectly, at least in the driver's mind. "You hurt, buddy? Oh, you are, aren't you? I'm sorry about that. I tried to stop, but I didn't see you until I was too close."

The driver touched the Lab's warm belly, and Golden Eyes returned the kind gesture by nuzzling the man's arm and giving him a gentle swipe of his tongue, whimpering sweetly.

"You're a good boy, aren't you? Why you out here all by yourself on this road? You lost?"

Golden Eyes did not respond, for he could not form human speech with his canine snout, but he yelped, barked, and inched closer to the driver. The man smelled of stale sweat, of booze. His body was thick, his shirt and jeans worn and threadbare, but he seemed nice enough.

"Don't you worry, boy. I won't let you die out here. Leether Holland ain't no mean SOB. I'll get you in my truck and next stop, we'll try to find you some help, okay?"

Golden Eyes whimpered and allowed himself to be picked up and carried to the cab.

"Jesus, you're heavier than you look."

Of course, I am twice the size that you see.

Without making it look suspicious, Golden Eyes used as much strength as he could to make it easier for Leether to help him into the cab. One, two good pushes, and he was in. He yelped once more to make the deception convincing and then staggered over into the passenger seat.

Leether shut the door behind him. "Okay, here we go. Don't you worry none, my little chocolate buddy. We'll get you all healed up. I'll have to get these damned brakes looked at too. That's the hardest I've ever had to stop, but it's all good. We'll get you all patched up. Don't you worry none."

Golden Eyes worried about many things the man could not conceive, but he settled into the chair and hoped that Leether would have more interesting things to say down the road. Texas was a long way off, and if he had to hear this smelly man ramble on and on about his 'chocolate buddy,' he'd go insane himself. But he was in the truck and on his way, and that mattered more than anything else right now. Soon, he'd be in Texas, and then…

"You know," Leether said, guiding the truck off the curb and back onto the road, "you remind me of a dog I used to have as a kid."

Golden Eyes whimpered.

Imagine that.

CORPUS CHRISTI, TEXAS

Chimalis always hesitated before knocking on Father Diego de Seña's door. It was protected by an antique owl-shaped knocker that always gave her the evil eye. *"Whooo…whoo…?"* it seemed to whisper as she drew near.

"Leave me alone," she said, grabbing its wrought-iron legs and lifting them to strike the door. "I'm in no *mooooood* today."

She announced her arrival with three sharp knocks that echoed on the other side of the thick Southern Live Oak door. A long pause, then the door opened slowly.

Father Diego de Seña greeted her with a thin smile. A short, old, and stooped man, he waved her in as if he were savoring the sweet scent of flowers. "Come in, my dear, come in. Forgive the mess. I so rarely have visitors, I forget to clean. "Come… come."

He stepped aside and let her in. She shut the door for him, then said, "Thank you for asking me to come, Father, but I'm confused as to why I'm here. I sent Luiz to bring you to me, not the other way around."

He chuckled in a half-hearted cough-laugh combination as he led her through the foyer and into the hall. "So impatient… Never fear, Chimalis, my dear. You'll know the reason soon enough."

Father de Seña had retired from the Diocese of Corpus Christi a little over eight years ago, but his service to the Bureau was still ongoing and invaluable in Chimalis' mind. As extensive as it was, the library she'd inherited was by no means complete; Father de Seña filled in the paranormal gaps, so to speak. The scars visible on his face—and his psyche—spoke volumes of his personal experience with many Cryptid baddies.

Father de Seña led her into his kitchen, where Luiz sat at a table, staring in wonder at the scores of tiny crosses—gold, silver, stone, and wooden ones—that he had acquired over the years. Covering nearly every open space on the wall, they were his protection against the dark and evil powers of the world, as he had explained to Chimalis more than once. Their presence seemed to work. When in his home, nothing horrific had ever happened to Chimalis, even when the supernatural baddies were in pursuit, which was actually the case sometimes. She was confident that they would be safe in Father de Seña's kitchen.

"I should have warned you about Father de Seña's love for crosses, Louie," she said with a wink. "It borders on neurotic."

"Hey," Father de Seña said, "a retired priest needs all the protection he can get. The baddies always seem to come after us the most."

"Yes, but so many?" Luiz's question sounded like a child seeing piles of snow for the first time.

Father de Seña shook his head and shot a glance at Chimalis. "He's new to this Cryptid scene, isn't he?"

Chimalis nodded. "Yes, but he's learning. Now, can we get on with it? Why am I here?"

Father de Seña nodded and offered Chimalis a chair at the table. "Would you like some coffee or tea?"

Chimalis nodded. "Tea would be fine. Thank you."

She sat and watched him as he prepared the tea.

Father de Seña's stoop and malformed back was what they called Dowager's Hump. Kyphosis was the more clinical term, but the old priest carried his affliction well. Chimalis thought he looked like Igor from the Frankenstein legend. He was in his eighties; she did not know his age exactly, nor was he inclined to reveal it. He moved reasonably well for an old man, she had to admit, though she could tell that his right hand shook a little, and he had a large bruise across the knuckles.

Luiz scrambled to his feet and moved to help.

"Back off, young man," Father de Seña said, waving him away. "The day I can't pour tea in my own home is the day I die. Now, go fetch that book we talked about and give your boss a look-see at its contents."

While Luiz went to fetch the *book*, the old priest prepared the tea. It took a while, a couple mumbled prayers beneath his breath, and a few gestures across his chest, but Father de Seña managed to pour three cups, sprinkle some lemon and sugar in each, and carry them all over to the table on a tray with an image of the Virgin Mary etched on the bottom.

Luiz returned, carrying a book encased in a leather sleeve. He sat down and laid the book carefully on the table. Chimalis motioned for Father de Seña to sit as well.

"Sit down, Father," she said, accepting her cup and taking a small sip. Steam from the hot liquid tickled her nose. "Tell me *why* you've asked me to come."

Father de Seña chuckled. It sounded more like a whisper, a raspy exhalation of air. "Poor Bluebird always in a hurry, never taking the time to stop, breathe, and reflect. Before I die, I want you to promise me that you will take some time for yourself once in a while, time for reflection. Life is not always about work and duty, you know."

I was just about to go on a damn vacation, Chimalis thought but didn't dare speak. No reason to, anyway. The old priest wouldn't consider a week or two off on a beach or in a mountain cabin a time for serious "reflection." She knew what Father de Seña wanted. He wanted her to retire, to get out of the Bureau, out of the VPA business, before her duty to it found her dead.

Chimalis nodded like she had done many times in his presence to humor him. It was an empty promise, but it would get them past the pleasantries and on to the matter at hand. "Yes, I promise. I will take time to reflect."

"And begin to believe in something greater than yourself?"

That was a new one, and frankly, a little insulting. She did believe in something greater than herself; otherwise, she would not have joined the FBI, nor would she be putting her life on the line every time she answered the Bureau's call to investigate VPA. *How dare he suggest that I —*

She sighed. "I promise. Now, can we get on with it?"

Father de Seña took a deep sip of his tea, seemingly unharmed by the hot liquid as it trickled down his throat. He finished his tea, crossed his chest, cleared his throat, and said, "Luiz... show her the book."

Luiz took the book and withdrew it from its leather binding. Then, with shaking hands, he laid it back on the table.

Chimalis' eyes grew wide, and she leaned away from the tome. "My god... that isn't what I think it is... is it?"

"What do you think it is?" Father de Seña asked.

She reached her hand out to it and then pulled it away quickly. "*De Bibliis Maledictione.* The Bible of Curses?"

"Correct." Father de Seña gestured to it. "Open it."

Chimalis shook her head. "I'm not touching it."

"Why? It's just a book."

"Yeah. Just a book wrapped in the skin of a black slave."

The legend had it that three *De Bibliis Maledictiones* had been printed and bound in skin.

Sometime in the seventeenth century, as the legend went, a ghost slave ship from Africa floated into the Spanish port of Cartagena. Everyone on board had been killed, mutilated in fact, their bodies (both Africans and crew alike) strung up on the masts to dangle like fruit from a tree. Only three Africans survived, still chained in the hold. When they were found, they were accused of the crime and put to death, although no one could give a convincing explanation as to how three chained, malnourished, and frightened Angolan boys could have committed such a despicable act. That did not seem to matter to the local Inquisition, so they were executed, and their skins used to cover a so-called "definitive" book on curses. Chimalis had assumed that all three volumes had been destroyed due to the despicable nature of their creation. Apparently not.

"I acquired it twenty years ago from a Peruvian monk," Father de Seña said, "who claimed that it was the very first copy of the three. I can't confirm that, nor could he, but there it is: the answer to your questions."

"And what questions are those?" she asked.

Father de Seña shook his head as if he were more than a little confused. "The questions that made you send young Luiz here to me."

"The creature—or creatures, actually—we are seeking, Chimalis," Luiz said, leaning into the conversation, "are two brothers from El Salvador, and they were cursed—"

"I'm aware of the legend," Chimalis said. She wrinkled her brow. "I found references to them in my library. Why did I have to come here to see this? Couldn't you have told me about its contents over the phone, or through Zoom, or something?"

"First of all," Father de Seña replied, waving off her question, "I don't *do* the internet. I'm too old for that silliness. And second, do you want to risk spooks and hackers online learning that The Bible of Curses still exists? Can you imagine the hell unleashed if the wrong people discovered its whereabouts?"

Chimalis nodded. He had a point there. "Okay, fair enough. But like I say, I know the legend. I found it among my father's books."

"But did his scholarship contain the full story of the legend," Father de Seña asked, "the name of what you seek, and the actual curse itself?"

Chimalis paused, considered, then, "In fact, no. It told of the two brothers and what they had done to raise the ire of the magician, who then cursed them for all time. It provided a physical description that matches the description from Officer Torres. The rest of the description had been obscured by a staining liquid. Something had been spilled on the book; coffee, perhaps. I couldn't make anything else out. The only other thing I found was some notes that my father had scribbled into the margins. The words "chains" and "El Mozote." They mean anything to you?"

Luiz nodded. "Well, the Spanish word for 'chain' is *cadena*. The name of the cursed brothers, Chimalis, is *El Cadejo*, and sometimes, the legend has it that they carry loose chains around their necks and ankles as a symbol of their eternal bondage."

"The *legend* is all over the place if you want the truth of it," Father de Seña said, rising with a groan from his chair to put his cup in the sink. "Each Central American country has its own variation, which I suspect is derived from chance glimpses, personal encounters with the creatures, and basic hearsay. Some claim to have seen chains, and others have not. Some accounts have one of the brothers being a white wolf, while the other is black. The black one is most often the evil one, although the white one has been known to be evil in some accounts. Regardless of color, the one that is *not* evil is said to help and sometimes protect people from harm, like poor drunks heading home on dangerous streets. But you know as well as I do that all cultures place their folklore in the context of their own social circumstances. The *essence* of each legend, however, is almost always true. The facts are coming together, Chimalis: the two brothers cursed in El Salvador nearly two centuries ago still exist. They are *Los Cadejos*, and I suspect they are both in the States, somewhere, right now."

Somewhere nearby too, Chimalis was certain. Not in Corpus Christi. Chimalis did not know why she was certain of that, but the east coast of Texas didn't feel like the place that the wolf/goat creature that had leapt from the back of the eighteen-wheeler filled with border-crossers would go. It was headed somewhere else. And where was its brother, the second one? Were they working together? At odds? Still, so many questions to answer.

"There is something else you need to know, boss," Luiz said, his tone turning serious. "Depending upon the legend, there are three types of evil *cadejo*.

"One legend in *De Bibliis Maledictiones* describes the evil one as the offspring of a normal dog and a *cadejo*. It isn't very violent, but it often deals with threats by turning them insane. The next is a regular *cadejo*, an evil dog. It acts like a werewolf, tearing into its victims with great savagery. The third is frequently described as a big, wounded dog bound in red-hot chains. Like the dog-*cadejo* hybrid, it too can drive threats mad. But this third one, boss, is most often referred to as… as…"

"Oh, stop stalling, Luiz," Father de Seña said, returning to the table and leaning on it as if he were exhausted. He probably was, Chimalis figured. The man, though still sharp of mind, was tired. She could see it in his eyes, his stance, and in the way he gulped air. "Your boss never wants to be spared or protected from the evils of the world, so don't protect her. Say it plain."

Luiz cleared his throat, swallowed, and said in a much lower volume, "The third one is the Devil, Chimalis. Satan himself."

Chimalis closed her eyes, leaned back into her chair, and breathed deeply to calm herself. *The Devil… oh goody!*

Chapter Six

The green Ford pickup pulled over, and Red Eyes jumped out of the bed. If he had human hands, he would have waved appreciation to the driver who now rummaged through his glove compartment to find a knife to cut his own throat. *Just as well*, Red Eyes thought, as he jumped a fence to a gated community while the driver drew the blade across the soft skin of his neck. *The man wasn't much of a human being anyway.*

What lovely houses! Red Eyes had never seen such beautiful little houses, all tucked in a row. Large, one-family homes bought and owned by equally useless human beings. That wasn't entirely fair, for surely amidst this ocean of wealth and privilege, there was at least one, perhaps two, families that he could point to as decent.

But not the family whose house he drew toward right now. It lay further back in the community, where the really rich folk lived, in tall, thick brick houses too large for their needs, with the kind of opulence that he hadn't experienced often in his life, at least not in the more rural places that he and his brother had lived those many, many years ago.

He felt his brother's presence now more than at any time in his search. Miguel was still far away, but he was drawing closer. *He knows I'm here*, Red Eyes thought, as he clopped down the center of the dark street that wound its way through the well-manicured homes. *And he's coming to pay me a visit.*

It was near midnight, and everyone in this quaint little community was asleep. Well, most everyone.

Where the cul-de-sac turned left, there was a stone house with the rear security light turned on. Red Eye could smell fear, anger, humiliation. He had smelled it from miles away as he and the now-dead good ol' boy in the green pickup had entered the city of Abilene. This was the kind of fear and humiliation that Red Eyes couldn't resist. *Miguel is coming, and I need all the strength I can muster to face him.*

Red Eyes jumped the faux-wooden fence that separated the house from its neighbors, then quietly, in shadow, made his way through a maze of newly-purchased swing sets, jungle-gyms, forgotten soccer balls, and even a wet teddy bear that one of the young ones in the house had forgotten to bring inside. Poor kid. By morning, he (or she) would have more to worry about than a soggy stuffed animal.

Red Eyes crept to the window. He reared up, placing his front hooves on the windowsill to peer inside. Beautiful house, indeed. A kitchen with all the modern amenities. Open-plan design with an attached dining room that rivaled the greatest kingly courts in all the world. Crystal chandelier hanging from a foyer that he wished he stood in right now. Plush living room furnishings that he could see from his vantage point.

A middle-aged woman came into the kitchen. She was distraught, sad, upset, terrified, all the things that Red Eyes loved to see and feel. She banged around in the kitchen as if preparing to make dinner. Red Eyes licked his dark lips.

A younger woman came in shortly thereafter. Half the other woman's age. Beautiful red hair flowing to the middle of her back. Green eyes. Perky breasts beneath a slim black top. *Does she have a bra on? Probably not.* The older woman, likely the mother of the child who had left the teddy bear in the yard, threw sharp glances at the young woman, trying to be helpful in the kitchen. The older woman did her best to contain her anger and rage, but the situation was too much. She banged pots, clapped plates, and before too long, she and the young piece of fluff were arguing about something Red Eyes could not hear, but it was clear from their body language, their radiated body heat, that they were not friends. The younger woman was not the sister or relative of the older woman. *She's a threat.*

The argument persisted, and a man walked in. He wore a grey suit. He was a lawyer just arrived from a case, or a doctor maybe. He certainly stank of professionalism, but Red Eyes could tell right away that in personality and behavior, he was less of a man than the bled-out fellow back in the Ford. This guy was a royal piece of work.

The man was clean-shaven. Tall. A hundred-dollar haircut; a thousand-dollar suit. A wrapped gift lay in his hand. He placed the gift and his suit coat on the table and jumped into the fight between the two women. He gently pushed the younger one toward the kitchen table. He rudely pushed the older one away, such that she fell back against the shiny metal sink with a thud. He cursed her loudly, calling her names that Red Eyes had heard far too often in such situations. The older woman fired back, and she dared to move closer. He yelled at her again and raised his hand as if he would strike her. The younger woman intervened and grabbed his arm, and slowly talked him down.

Finally, he turned to the younger one and wrapped her in his arms. *Get a room*, Red Eyes thought as he watched them engage in a passionate kiss that made the older woman, now recovered and standing there watching, want to cry. The man pulled away from the younger woman and handed her the gift. She beamed with happiness, and then together, they walked away, leaving the older woman standing there in humiliated silence.

Now the older woman broke down and sobbed. Red Eyes could feel her anger, her fear. But there was something else there too, something he prefered in her emotions, that *thing* that he craved in all situations like this.

Revenge.

He stretched a little higher and tapped his hoof on the window. The woman noticed. First, she started, shocked and afraid that there was someone at the window looking in. When she saw that it was a wolf—or, seemed to be a wolf from where she was standing — she paused and showed surprise. She even smiled a little.

Come to me, Red Eyes said to her through her confused mind. *Come, and tell me your story.*

She grabbed a chair from the dining room table, turned it around to sit in front of the window, and then stared into Isai's red eyes.

She told him her story. It was a longer story than necessary, but Red Eyes let her go on and on, and among the woman's confused droplets of memories, a picture emerged.

Two years ago, her highly professional husband (the man making kissy-face with the young redhead) had gone off to a banking conference in Dallas. He'd always been an abusive man, at least verbally, but upon his return, it turned physical. First, just shoving, then the occasional slap across the face. She had contemplated leaving and filing for divorce, but his money and his house was too sweet a deal to just throw away, especially now that they had two kids. She could endure it, she had thought. She could work around the edges, stay in an acceptable lane, and all would be well.

Then the redhead showed up one night. Her husband had said she was a manager at a local bank and that she had come over to discuss a set of equity loans he was proposing that she begin to offer in her branch. A nice, pleasant dinner, and they did indeed "talk shop." But there was something else there, something on the edge of their pleasant conversation that the wife had picked up. Too many occasions of having their hands cross paths: both reaching for the butter or the wine bottle. Too many giggly laughs at nothing. Too many quick looks in each other's direction. The young, and very attractive young lady, left after dinner, and that was that. But not so fast.

Redhead came over again, and then again, and finally, one day, as the wife pulled the BMW into their two-car garage, her husband met her at the car and told her he had hired the girl to be the kids' nanny. There was no need for that, the wife told her husband, for she was a stay-at-home mom and why waste the money? That didn't matter to the husband. The deal was done.

But Pretty Redhead was no nanny.

It started slowly. Nothing for the first week or so. And then her husband would sneak out of their bed late at night, sometimes two or three in the morning. The "nanny's" bedroom was on the second floor, just down the hall from the kids' room. Squeak, squeak, squeak… on and on and on. Quieter at first, but after she had said nothing about it for a week, it got louder and louder and rougher until the children started to ask her what was going on. What was Daddy doing in Miss Rachael's room?

Finally, she confronted her husband, who, of course, brushed it off and told her if she didn't approve, too bad. "Try to divorce me," he barked at her, threatening to hit her in front of the kids. "Try it and see what you get."

So that is the way of it now. She kept her mouth shut while her husband and the "nanny" continue to have an open affair right in front of her, the kids, and God himself. From the beginning, the redhead had tried to make peace, tried to contribute to the house chores, and she did work with the kids from time to time, as if she was their mother. It became too much. Too much pain, humiliation for the wife to keep going on this way. Something had to give. But what? What could she do without jeopardizing herself, her children, and her opulent lifestyle?

I know a way out of the madness, Red Eyes said through her misery as she stared deeply into his eyes. *Come, open the door, and I will show you…*

She opened the door, and Red Eyes walked in.

He shot a quick glance around the kitchen. His gaze fell across the gondola countertop which separated the kitchen from the dining room.

There, as pretty as you pleased, sat a knife block with four gunmetal gray handles sticking out.

"No," she said, resisting at first. Red Eyes reiterated his commitment to her happiness. "Okay," she whispered finally, "if you think it'll help."

Oh, it will, it will… Red Eyes was adamant in his assurances, and so she pulled the thickest, heaviest, largest knife from the block, which, ironically, had been purchased by the fluff upstairs that was being taken like a beast by her husband at the expense of her happiness.

She held the knife as Red Eyes directed, firm and forward in her grip. She breathed deeply and let the sounds of their lovemaking guide her upstairs. The kids were in their rooms, she figured, these days trying to just stay quiet and invisible. That was good. They didn't need to be a part of all this.

Red Eyes followed her up the stairs. When they reached the top, she looked at him once more, as if again uncertain of the wisdom of this idea. He reassured her again by blasting images of her husband's abuse and affair through her tangled thoughts, and he reminded her that a man's abuse rarely is confined to the wife. *Soon, your children will feel the sting of his slaps. Act now, while you still have time.*

She needed no further goading. Her mind was set, and she was so happy that she had come up with the idea all by herself. Finally, she was showing some self-control, taking agency over her life, her happiness. She felt good. She was doing the right thing.

Red Eyes followed her down the hall and then stopped. She didn't need him anymore, and besides, he wasn't hungry, not for flesh anyway. From where he waited, he would receive everything he required.

The wife stumbled toward the door. The noise inside the room reached its climax. She paused just outside, breathed deeply again, and then turned the knob counter-clock.

The adulterers began to scream as the wife made her statement of liberation and freedom proudly. Red Eyes focused on her speech, slash after slash, stab after stab until the pain in her heart flowed out like water. He accepted the pain—hers and her husband's and his lover's. It flowed out of the room like twisted red ropes of ethereal fog. It slid through the air and into his body, through his red eyes that pulsed now like lanterns in a cave. And it gave him the vision and the strength that he needed for the last leg of his long, arduous journey.

Soon, Miguel, Red Eyes thought as the wife finished her work, and he shivered with power. *Soon we will meet, and you will pay for your crimes.*

VAUGHN, NEW MEXICO

Leether Holland tried climbing into his truck, but Golden Eyes stopped him.

"Whas'a matter you, boy?" Leether asked, his speech slurred and his breath stagnant with whiskey and bean burrito. "Why you actin' like thisss?"

Golden Eyes sat in the driver's seat of Leether's semi, and he wasn't budging. The man was drunk, and no matter how long the trip had been or how many more miles they had to travel, he would not let this man drive. The *curse* wouldn't allow Golden Eyes to let Leether drive. Golden Eyes had fought against his inclination to protect travelers, drunks like this man, from falling to an ill fate, but the curse could not be denied. It was his duty now, regardless of circumstances or his situation, to protect drunks. If he let this man drive, he'd be dead in an hour, if not sooner. Leether was in no shape to get behind the wheel.

Over the years, Golden Eyes had wondered why the magician had cursed him with the instinctual need to protect drunks and others inebriated or incapacitated in some manner or other. Isai had not been so bound by compassion and desire to do right by people. But then again, Isai had been cursed with dark, dangerous inclinations, which fit his core personality well. The curse had manifested itself in two distinct ways, but which of them had gotten the short draw of the stick? Golden Eyes wondered. Was it worse to always burn with a desire to help people or to harm them? Neither urge had helped the poor people of El Mozote, had it?

Leether staggered back from the door in fear of Golden Eyes' incessant growling. "You've gotten real cocky since Carrizozo. Perhaps I'll just let you go n' not worry about it, hmm?"

Not long after Leether had picked him up, Golden Eyes had started feeling better. An hour into their trip, he sat upright with no pain. Shortly thereafter, he pretended to need food. Well, not pretend *per se*, but played to the expectations of this man who couldn't tell the difference between Golden Eyes and a dog he once had as a child. By the time they had reached Carrizozo, Golden Eyes had mended completely.

Golden Eye stood his ground and placed an idea into Leether's mind. The man scratched his head, rubbed his sweaty face, and said, "I guessn' you right. I ain't in no shape to drive. Fine, fine… I'll climb into the back n' sleep it off. Stop your damned belly achin'."

Satisfied, Golden Eyes moved to allow the man to get in. Leether clambered into the back of the cab, where he kept a small rollaway mattress, smelly sheet, and lumpy pillow for those occasions when he needed to pull over and crash for a few hours. The man cursed and grumbled and groused until he had successfully made it into his sleeping space. He said curse words Golden Eyes had never heard before, but finally, he gave way to his affliction and buried his head into the lumpy pillow. He was snoring in five minutes.

Golden Eyes stood down. He jumped over to the passenger's seat, turned round and round to press his hooves into the cracked leather covering to make the seat comfortable, and then lay down himself.

Despite his miraculous recovery, he still needed rest and time to think. Brother Isai drew close now.

Still in Texas, of course, but it had become clear that he was moving in a north, northwesterly manner. Exactly where Red Eyes headed was unclear. Perhaps he did not have a particular destination in mind.

Golden Eyes perked his ears. Intriguing notion. Perhaps he could use their spirit connection to influence his brother. Golden

Eyes need only determine the place he wanted them to meet. And if he got there first, well then, he could prepare the ground for the inevitable: confronting Red Eyes and settling their dispute once and for all.

It was a drunk who had sparked the disaster at El Mozote. History didn't record it that way, of course, but then, most historians had not been present at the time of the massacre, and hearsay and secondhand accounts were never fully accurate. Golden Eyes was there, as was Red Eyes. A drunk, plus a lot of misunderstanding, led to the massacre of nearly a thousand souls on that day. *I was trying to help them, to save them.*

No, that wasn't entirely true.

I was trying to save one drunk, one lousy drunk… and I sparked a massacre.

No. He couldn't think of it in such stark terms. He couldn't blame himself, for that was Red Eyes' job. But neither he nor Red Eyes could be held responsible for what the curse demanded of them. Could they? Did they have free will? Could they fight against the imperatives that were placed upon them when that ex-slave and magician raised his dry, knobby, and grotesque fingers and cursed them for all eternity?

Yes… and no.

On that day in December Nineteen Eighty-One, both he and Red Eyes had made choices, and neither one fully resisted their natures. They let the curse flow through their actions and inactions, and many, many died. A reckoning was coming, Golden Eyes knew. But where?

As Leether snored in his fitful, drunken sleep, Golden Eyes studied the road map on the passenger-side floorboard. He put his hooves down to help spread the map out so that he could get a better look. The curse had given him the sight of a wolf and thus, in the proper light, he could see very well, though he did not understand all the symbols and lines on this human map. None of it made much sense to him, though he could make out the solid border line between New Mexico and Texas, and he knew that

Leether was hauling his goods into Texas, for he had mentioned it again and again.

Golden Eyes leaned over the seat and let his muzzle sniff the paper. Truck oil smell, with a touch of gin, whiskey. A part of the map had been saturated with spilled coffee and burrito stains, and there was a smear of hardened ketchup near a corner. Golden Eyes licked the dry ketchup and felt his stomach rumble. He was hungry, and what little scraps Leether tossed to him as they had made their way across New Mexico were insufficient, for he knew that Red Eyes was gaining strength by killing and driving to madness all those who crossed his path. That was Red Eyes' special nature. That was what the curse had done to him. For Golden Eyes, the urge to kill, to terrorize, to drive people mad was less so. Thus, he had to find other ways to find food, to draw strength. And he had to find it soon, he knew, for they drew near the final destination.

Close to a small stain of grease, Leether had circled in pencil a town in Texas. Golden Eyes squinted to make out the name of the town.

L-U-B-B-O-C-K.

Yes, that was where they were headed, and that was where he and Red Eyes would meet.

He'd give Leether four hours to sleep, and then he'd wake him up. And then, they'd roll out and make Lubbock, Texas, before Red Eyes got there.

Chapter Seven

After Corpus Christi, they returned to San Antonio to check the FBI's mainframe, per her request to Luiz. It had kicked out three possible directions that their *cadejo* was likely to go, assuming that he was catching rides.

From San Antonio, he could have taken I-10 toward El Paso or East toward Houston. He could have taken I-35 through Austin and on up to Dallas. Or he could be avoiding the interstate system altogether and working through the heart of the state, up 281, 183, 87, and potentially others. That way would lead him toward Abilene and points north, northwest.

Chimalis had already thrown out the possibility of an eastward move. It just didn't feel likely, especially if it was seeking its wolf-goat brother. Nothing east in the state would allow such a creature to thrive for long without drawing the attention of local VPA agents. The other routes were all viable, but none of them spoke to Chimalis as definitive. So, Luiz's search helped but didn't answer the key question: where were the *cadejo* going? The only course of action now was to dream.

To help with that, Chimalis called an old friend.

The Zuni priest on the other end of the Zoom meeting wasn't happy with Chimalis' idea. "I've never put anyone into a trance through the internet, Chimalis. It's not my style. Can we not at least meet in Albuquerque or Santa Fe?"

Chimalis shook her head, making sure she was in the frame of her tablet so that the man could clearly see her face. "No. *El Cadejo* is somewhere near, but it's on the move. I cannot leave San

Antonio now — or Texas for that matter — until I know where it's going and what it's fully capable of doing. It has to be this way. And there are two of them. I have to try to find the other. Where the one is, the other will go. Do you understand?"

Halian nodded and gave a big sigh that came across Chimalis' earbuds like a hurricane. She winced. "I don't like this, girl. You should be surrounded by support, people of your own kind, helping you on this journey. That's the Zuni way."

Individual vision quests, or trying to commune with the spirits alone, were frowned upon by many Zuni priests. Contacting the spirits, and in many cases, Kachina, was a matter for the entire community. She knew that, but there was no time for the proper protocols to be observed. "I know, and if my mother were still alive, she'd tan my hide." Chimalis smirked, remembering her mother's awkward attempts at corporal punishment when Chimalis, as a little girl, had been found with her hand in the candy jar... or whatever other indiscretion that was considered unacceptable behavior. Mother was a lover, not a fighter. She preferred hugs over spankings.

"I trust you, Halian. You're a good priest. You're a good representative of our people. Let's get on with it."

He sighed again. "Very well, but I will not be responsible for failure or for any psychic damage you may experience. The dream world is wondrous, Chimalis, but it is also dangerous. You contact the wrong spirit, honey, and you may not survive it. Do you understand? I need to hear you say that you understand."

Chimalis nodded. "I understand... fully."

She had cleared out a space in the evidence locker room of the local FBI office. The lights were low, save for the glow of her tablet. She had prepared prayer sticks, with feather and shell fetishes dangling at random intervals, and had strung them up around her to create a kind of makeshift cocoon that resembled a dreamcatcher, just like her mother had done on occasion attempting to do the very same thing that Chimalis was now trying. Incense burned in a bowl near her crossed legs, and the rising smoke smelled like spring flowers; it soothed her frayed nerves.

She *was* nervous. Very much so. But this had to be done. The time of playing cat-and-mouse with this hooved, wolf-like monster roaming through Texas on a killing spree was over.

"Okay, Chimalis. Close your eyes, breathe deeply, and listen to my instructions…"

She did as directed, letting all of her anxiety, fear, and anger flow from her body with each breath. As much as she was able to release, that is. She never gave it all away, for she had learned long ago that to be a good VPA agent, one had to always maintain a little anxiety, a little fear. Those who did not fear the spirit world and its supernatural powers were doomed to suffer, and perhaps die, by it. She had been lucky so far, and she had every intention of surviving a physical encounter with *El Cadejo*, whenever and wherever their meeting occurred.

Halian's voice was soft, sincere. He was a man in his seventies, and technically not the most qualified person from the Zuni reservation in New Mexico to conduct this dream trance. He was a Priest of the Bow, which, these days, did not mean the same thing it did back in the eighteenth and nineteenth centuries. He still concerned himself with matters of conflict and war, but in his official capacity, he served more as a librarian and a scholar for the Zuni people than he did a warrior priest. His specialty was Zuni lore and custom. Halian was a family friend. He and her mother had grown up together.

Her skin tingled as she listened to the soft, Mondrian echo of Halian's voice over Zoom. Luckily, she was very tired, so reaching that point where consciousness ended, and sleep prevailed was easily achieved. Chimalis did not understand all of the Zuni language, which was unique among other Native American Pueblo communities in the southwestern United States. Her mother had taught her some of it, just enough to get by. Halian mixed in some English and even some Spanish. It didn't really matter to her what words he used. She focused on his tone, his pacing.

As she drifted, she thought of the case and all the evidence that she and Luiz had gathered so far. Not as much as she would have liked, and hopefully, this dream trance would help. It had to. The body count kept climbing, and time *was* running out.

She fell into her dream. It felt like that, like she was falling through the air toward something hard, like rock. She just kept falling and falling and falling, and Halian's voice persisted like dark matter, there but not visible, pushing and pulling her along, filling up the vacant space between herself and the world around her. The sensation reminded her of that late 1990's film *Contact*, where Jodie Foster fell through the wormhole. Chimalis fell through her dream, with the priest's voice guiding her.

She reached out with her thoughts, seeking the other *cadejo*, hoping that she could make a connection. She had no idea where it was or even what to say if she found it. Could it be talked to? Could it be reasoned with? She didn't think so, at least not in the manner she needed, but what choice did she have? She focused on Halian's voice and searched for the beast.

Miles and miles of blacktop poured through her mind as if she were on a great sled sliding down a long slope. She turned her drifting thoughts toward the legend of the beast, remembering all she had read, all that Father de Seña had discovered. She imagined herself in El Salvador, mid-nineteenth century, one of two boys walking home and an aged magician giving them solace and shelter for the long night. She focused on that image and played the details out in her mind.

Beads of sweat gathered on her forehead, her cheeks, her neckline. The air around her wasn't particularly hot or humid, but the memories of being someone else nearly two centuries ago drove her body temperature and blood pressure high. She resisted the urge to wipe the sweat away and instead let it run down her face and drip from her chin. She squeezed her eyes shut and imagined herself being cursed by the magician.

In her mind, her body changed, like the two boys' bodies had done. Then, she was a wolf, a goat, both. It felt good. Senses that had been dulled by her human limitations and physiology now exploded through her body. She could hear everything, even the slightest whisper. She could hear Halian's stomach growl in hunger, discern every minor deviation in his breathing, every inflection in his words. She could hear the pipes in the walls of the room crack and groan as water ran through them, feel the room settle and expand with slight changes in barometric pressure. Her eyes remained closed, but she could see right through her lids.

In wolf form, she ran across a field. She could not tell which brother's eyes she looked through. It didn't seem to matter; all she felt was anger, shock, humiliation, all the residual feelings from when the magician turned them as they laughed and laughed and made their way down the long road from the magician's home and hospitality. But was it his fault entirely? Didn't the brothers share in the blame? Wasn't it Isai who had coerced his brother Miguel into taking those things? Wasn't it Isai who had —

Now she had their names: Isai and Miguel. But which was which?

"Isai," she whispered. The name echoed through her mind. "Are you there, Isai? Are you there?"

No answer. She tried again and again. Nothing. Like a wall of pure darkness, no sound, shape, movement. Nothing.

"Miguel?"

Chimalis paused, was about to say the name again, and then she got a tickle. A thread of thought leached its way into her mind like a line of floss pulled between teeth. The thread picked up stray images from her case and put them into an order that she did not, at first, understand. Then clarity emerged.

A decade of just dealing with the reality of the change and the fact that they were no longer human, but some malformed beasts from the twisted, angry mind of an ex-slave.

Then tentative acceptance, as family and friends rejected and expunged you from their collective memories.

Saving your brother Isai from an angry mob, and then, against your nature, turning them all insane as a diversion for escape.

Then trying to live a quiet, humble life in the jungles of El Salvador, Guatemala, Honduras, and Nicaragua. Trying to fall into acceptable routines so that you did not frighten the local peoples such that they raised a mob to find and kill you. And having to constantly fall back on your worst instincts to keep yourself alive, for part of the curse gave you an insatiable need for survival, even when you fought against such instincts and tried to die.

Year after year, decade after decade. Until the first century was gone, and you became restless and angry that nothing would ever change. And what were your choices then?

One last effort to find peace. Travel through Costa Rica, Panama, Columbia, and the very edge of Amazonia to find solace at last. Until Isai… poor, misguided Isai, could no longer live without human contact, would never give in to the curse and accept the new life as a wolf, a goat. Isai began to turn villagers mad just for sport, giving them subtle urges to kill their friends, families, even themselves. Taking comfort and strength through their suffering.

And then a long, long journey back north, again through Panama, Costa Rica, and finally to El Salvador, back home, where everyone you ever loved and knew were gone. And everywhere you go, every place you touch, the legend, the fear of who, of what you are, grows. Isai's a black wolf. Miguel's a white. There are chains hanging from your neck and legs. Isai's the white wolf; Miguel the black. Lies and hearsay all of it, but a nugget of truth within every twist of the legend. You are a wolf. You are a goat. You are evil.

Then, finally, El Mozote. Nineteen Eighty-One. The image now is fuzzy, muddled. Miguel's emotions clouding Chimalis' clear understanding of what happened there a couple weeks before Christmas. All she could see were villagers, scores and scores of them. Gunfire, violence, rage, blood, death. All happening at once in her mind, as seen through the eyes of a boy turned wolf-goat. Bright, golden eyes.

"Let me help you," Chimalis whispered, her heart beating fast and hard in her ears. "Help me find your brother."

You don't need his help, another voice said, breaking through the soupy madness of El Mozote. *I will guide you myself. Come… and see.*

Chimalis opened her eyes. The toothy muzzle of a wolf, its red eyes pulsing bright like lamplight, stared back at her.

Come and see…

It opened its mouth, bared its fangs, and leapt at her throat through the dream.

Chimalis screamed, fell back, and hit her head on the bare floor.

She awoke in an emergency room bed, with wires attached to her right arm. A nasal cannula lay under her nose. She tore that off immediately and sat up. She panicked for a moment, her mind still confused with after-images of her dream trance. She reached over to tear the wires from her arm. Luiz stopped her.

"No, no, Chimalis," he said, holding her arm back as she struggled. "It's okay. You're fine. You're in the hospital. They're monitoring your vitals while they run some tests. It's okay."

She fought against him for a few seconds longer, then relaxed. Her head ached, and not just because of the big bump on the back that she now could feel through her hair; she had a screaming headache that she knew was from Isai, from Red Eyes, trying to leap at her through the dream, to sink his fangs into her throat. Not to kill her. No. But to leave his mark so that, no matter where he was, she could track him, find him. Chimalis quickly touched her neck. She breathed a sigh of relief. No fang marks. Then she felt disappointment.

He should have bitten me. I should have allowed it.

But she didn't really need that kind of mark, that kind of "connection" with *El Cadejo*, for the other one, Golden Eyes, had slipped in the name of the place where they were going, right before she struck her head on the evidence room floor.

Chimalis rubbed her neck. "How long have I been here?"

"A few hours," Luiz said. "We're just waiting on some blood work, a final assessment of the CT scan of your noodle. Make sure your concussion isn't serious."

"It's a concussion?"

Luiz nodded. "That's what they said. The doctor will return soon to tell us everything."

Chimalis nodded. "We need to get out of here, Louie. I know where we have to go."

Luiz's mood brightened. "You found them? It?"

"Yes."

She told him as much as she remembered through the throbbing pain in her head, the drowsiness, the dizziness. Some of the details were missing. The in-a-flash story of their lives from the first moment of the curse to the present was incomplete, and the biggest part missing was El Mozote.

Chimalis reached toward Luiz's satchel lying on a chair near her bed. "Lend me your tablet, Louie. We need to find out everything we can."

He pulled the tablet out of his satchel and handed it over. She blinked several times, shook her head to clear away the cobwebs, and did a Google search.

El Mozote came up right away. Early December, Nineteen Eighty-One. The El Salvadoran civil war raged, and elements from the government's Atlacati Battalion, designed for rapid response and deployment, entered the small town of El Mozote. They had clashed with guerilla forces nearby and so wanted to sweep the town to ensure that there were no insurgents working in the area. After the sweep, the villagers were instructed to stay in their homes and not come out, or they would be shot.

The next morning, the slaughter began. The government forces brought the villagers out of their homes, separated the women and children from the men, and systematically killed them all. It went on and on and on.

That was it. She searched for any explanation as to why the massacre occurred, as if government forces could justify such an atrocity in any meaningful way. She found none, save for an apology that the El Salvadoran government had given their people years later. Chimalis gritted her teeth. *Bastards!*

No explanation for the brutality, other than madness, and she knew that the cursed brothers had been involved. But how? And why? Miguel had tried telling her, tried to show her what had happened, but he had been interrupted by Isai, by Red Eyes, and there was nothing online, of course, that told her how *El Cadejo* had been involved. Obviously, nobody knew of their involvement. Only three entities in the entire world knew: the brothers themselves and her.

The most logical explanation was that Red Eyes had driven the government soldiers mad, and perhaps Golden Eyes had tried to stop him. However, thinking back to her psychic link with Miguel, Chimalis didn't think that that was quite right. Indeed, they were involved, but the circumstances were more complicated than that, as real life almost always was. The brothers had been involved with El Mozote. That was clear. But how, and to what extent?

"Say," Luiz said, getting that inquisitive look on his face when he searched his mind for an obscure detail, "didn't you once tell me that your father worked a combined US-British VPA operation in Central America back in the Eighties?"

Chimalis now searched *her* thoughts. It was difficult to remember everything her father and mother had done over their long careers, but yes, as she knew well, her father had been in Guatemala and Honduras roughly around that same time. He had been all over Central and South America back in the late Seventies, early Eighties.

Her heart sank. *And he had scribbled* 'El Mozote' *in the margins of the book in the library.* "Yes, Louie, he did. But I have no details about his activities there."

"Do you think he might have encountered *El Cadejo* while there?"

I'm certain of it now. She shrugged. "I don't know. Maybe. But as I say, I've no details about his missions, so we must act on what we know." She swallowed to clear her throat. "Is the good priest on his way?"

"Yes. His plane lands at San Antonio International in about two hours."

Chimalis nodded. "Good. Then call that damn doctor in to say his piece, and then let's get out of here. We've got a plane of our own to catch."

"Yes, sir." Luiz was about to leave the room. Then he paused, turned, and asked, "Where are we going?"

"Lubbock."

Luiz scowled. He looked like he had just bitten into a sour grape. "Damn… I hate Lubbock."

Chapter Eight

The human woman who had reached out to him through her dreams was coming. He had done the best he could to prepare her for the inevitable, imparting to her as much information as he could about his and Isai's story, their history, before his brother had intervened and had attacked her. What troubled Golden Eyes about the experience was that Isai had not attacked to kill or drive her mad. He *wanted* her to find him, *wanted* her to come to Lubbock and see. *See what?* Golden Eyes wondered. The answer was clear. *Come to Lubbock to see her own death… and mine too.*

So she was coming, whoever she was. Law enforcement, for certain, but no law enforcement officer or entity had ever come close to killing Red Eyes or even subduing his actions. An entire battalion of El Salvadoran soldiers hadn't been able to do it. By Golden Eyes' recollection, there had been only one person who had even come close to killing Red Eyes: a British MI6 officer working undercover in the area of El Mozote, but even he, in the end, had been forced to withdraw. What could this one human woman do to change the terrible events that had been put into motion decades ago?

So it came down to him, Golden Eyes, and what would he do when he faced his brother again? Red Eyes hadn't arrived yet, that was certain. But he was near. So near that Golden Eyes could not shake the sensation from his spine, which tingled with both excitement and fear. He hadn't seen his brother in almost thirty years. Regardless of the circumstances, regardless of the violence and death that he had had to endure in the company of Red Eyes for nearly two centuries, it would be nice to see him again. To stand before him and say, finally after all these many years that he —

Leether opened the cab door and climbed in. "Forgot the damned bill of lading. Can't unload cargo without that, now can we?"

The bill, attached to a clipboard, was sitting on the driver's seat. Leether grabbed it, and Golden Eyes leapt, much like Red Eyes had done in the woman's dream vision. He did not bite or scratch the man; he simply knocked Leether off his feet and onto the mixture of concrete and scattered gravel of the warehouse loading dock. Leether yelped in shock and pain. As they fell together onto the concrete, Golden Eyes made sure that the man's head did not strike the gravel. He didn't want to kill the man; Leether had been good to him. But it was time to leave, and there was no time for sad, teary goodbyes. He had to act before Leether closed the cab door and any opportunity to flee was lost.

"Where are you going?" Leether called to him. "Come back, buddy. Come back."

Golden Eyes paused and turned, compelled to reveal what he really was.

The expression on the truck driver's face was difficult to accept. Golden Eyes always hated finally revealing his true nature to innocents who had trusted him with kindness. *But you must see me now as I am*, he said through Leether's confused mind. *See me, and tell the woman I am here.*

He imparted to Leether all the knowledge he had of the woman who had reached out to him through her dream. He wanted to make sure that the man understood what he had to do now, who he had to contact to report his sighting of a wolf-goat thing. *Tell her, Leether*, Golden Eyes said. *Tell her what I am and where I've gone.*

Red Eyes wanted the woman to come and see. Very well; Golden Eyes would oblige. But he had arrived first, so now it was a matter of where to go and wait for his brother to find him.

Golden Eyes turned away from the terrified, confused trucker and disappeared into the dry brush.

A silver SUV turned into an abandoned parking lot. It stopped, the side door slid open, and Red Eyes jumped out.

The occupants of the SUV, a sweet family heading back to Tulsa after visiting relatives in Abilene, had graciously given him a lift. Now, they didn't even bother to shut the door behind him. The father put the vehicle back in drive, gunned the engine, and sped across the dark asphalt. The SUV was up to sixty before it struck one of the concrete lampposts in the parking lot. The vehicle burst into flames; no one tried to escape.

Red Eyes relished in the family's screams as they burned to death behind him. He paused a moment and shook himself, like a wet dog would do, and basked in the power that that sweet family's death had given him. It would be his last meal for a while, he knew. His last until his own reunion with his long-lost brother Miguel.

He was close now, so close. Where exactly, Red Eyes still did not know. But they were back together again, here, in Lubbock. Not the most ideal place to reunite, Red Eyes freely admitted. Too many people, too many chances for public interference of what he was about to do, what he needed to do. Too many things could go wrong in such a populated area.

In the end, it didn't matter. Red Eyes had a plan, one that he had devised during the long trip from Abilene, in the perpetual hug of the little boy in the back of the SUV that was now a-swirl with pitch-black smoke and red flame.

From the moment that he had felt that woman's presence, from the first word he had heard her say through her dream trance, he set his plan. He tried attacking her through the dream, to mark her with his teeth and know exactly where she was at any given time. But she was strong, quick. She had skills that Red Eyes hadn't seen or felt since El Mozote and that undercover agent working the jungles during the civil war. She was good, and Red

Eyes had failed in his efforts to mark her. She had reached out to his brother as well, and he was there, telling her everything, laying out his and Isai's fall into madness, into freakdom, into this perpetual hell from which they could never escape. And she was coming to find them both. Miguel had given her the name of their final meeting place, and she was coming. Not just her, but an entire team of people to help Miguel in his fight against his brother. *To fight me*, Red Eyes thought as he began his slow, deliberate clop through the heart of Lubbock. *To find me and to kill me. But they won't succeed, for I have a plan.*

Everyone he met, every person that mistook him for a sweet, lost poodle, was given a task: *rob that store over yonder; kill your father; run into the path of that speeding car; jump from that roof.* And on and on and on. By the time Red Eyes had walked a mile, police, firefighter, and EMT sirens blared across the city. After the second mile, he had done his duty.

Lubbock erupted into a chaotic mess that would last for days at least, if not longer. Red Eyes was pleased as he turned out of town and wandered down a quieter, more peaceful street toward his reunion with Miguel.

The woman and her team were closing in fast. The madness he had just wrought should slow her down, at least long enough for him to find his brother. Red Eyes was fine with her, in the end, finding them both. *Come and see* was the message he had given her through her dream, and so be it. It was a message from the Bible, from Revelations: *And I saw when the Lamb opened one of the seals, and I heard, as it were the noise of thunder, one of the four beasts saying, Come and see…*

She and her foolish lapdogs would bear witness to the greatest family reunion of all time.

Come and see, wherever you are. Come… and see.

Red Eyes howled and slipped into a patch of trees.

Riots were erupting everywhere as Chimalis, Luiz, and Father de Seña landed at Preston Smith International in their agency-issued commuter plane. The Texas National Guard had been called up and readied for crowd control. At least two dozen people had been injured in violence: five of which were serious, three of which were deaths. A curfew had been put into place. The city was on the edge of total collapse.

One freaking wolf did all this? It was hard for her to imagine. She had dealt with powerful Cryptids before, some even more personally violent, but nothing with the scope of this one. To drive so many mad all at once. *If left unchecked, what could it do?* The thought was terrifying.

They were rushed from PSI via bulletproof van to visit with a truck driver, Leether Holland, who was shaken up but otherwise mentally intact.

"I stared right at it," he said, his breath coming in short bursts. "It had golden eyes and was as big as a wolf. Damn it all, it was a wolf!"

Chimalis shook her head. "And you didn't notice that it was a wolf at any time during your trip across New Mexico?"

"Naw. Like I said, it reminded me of a chocolate lab I used to have." He sniffed as if he were crying. "He was nice, and I thought he was injured when I hit him, but he recovered so quickly, I couldn't believe it. I guess that should have given me a clue, but Mama Holland's boy ain't always the brightest, you know? I thought it was just a stray."

"Do you remember anything else strange about it?"

Leether shook his head. "Other than him changing right before my eyes, no, I — well, there was the odd behavior of not letting me drive while I was drunk. I thought that was strange. I never heard a dog do that before, but then, I haven't had too many pups with me on my trips. Good thing, too. If he hadn't done that, then I might not be here with you right now." He shook his head and smiled. "Good… good dog. Or whatever he is."

"Do you happen to know where it went?"

"Naw. It just lit out, in that direction." He pointed. "Just slipped away. Course, I was so damned scared at the time, and surprised. I wasn't thinking too clearly."

You're lucky you have a mind left at all, Chimalis wanted to say but kept quiet. What the trucker had said confirmed it: the *cadejo* that he had traveled with was the good one, or at least, the better of the two. She had little doubt about that as the man began his story, but it was always good to confirm these things. The good one had golden eyes; the bad one red. That was an important detail to have on hand, for in the heat of battle, two grey wolves might not look all that different from each other. She needed a good differentiation to work with to drive the dagger into the proper heart, the right wolf. If, of course, it came down to that.

She hugged her purse, the Zuni ritual knife nestled comfortably inside.

"Thank you, Mr. Holland, for the information. We very much appreciate it."

She turned away. Leether called to her. "Hey. You gonna kill it if you find it?"

Chimalis paused, looked at Luiz and Father de Seña, then said, "Yes. I will… if I have to."

Chimalis pulled out her knife and looked at it. *I will do what I have to do to make the madness stop.*

He never imagined himself choosing his gravesite, but here it was: a junkyard with piles upon piles of old cars, rotting tires, discarded home appliances, and all other manner of metal, plastic, and cardboard detritus that humans cast aside. He had imagined that his end would come in some thick forest in El Salvador, or Guatemala, or in a million other out-of-the-way places. At the hands of human beings who had grown angry and terrified of his and Isai's presence. But here he was, in the middle of a muddy graveyard, standing near a puddle of brown water, waiting for his brother to come into view and end this. End it all.

Red Eyes was nearby. So near now that Golden Eyes could smell him. The sweet, moldy smell of his damp fur. It had been a long, long time, and surprisingly, the smell did not scare him or fill him with the kind of dread he was expecting. It was his brother's smell, and it was neither an unfamiliar scent nor unwelcome.

I'm here, Golden Eyes said through his mind.

He reached out to Red Eyes and guided him forward the last mile. He reached out to the woman as well, though he did not know where she was or how close. She was near, he could tell, but she needed directions to his location.

Golden Eyes signaled to them both one final time, and then he stepped away from the puddle. He found a tall, stable pile of junk to put his back against.

Then he sat down, closed his eyes, and waited.

Chapter Nine

I'm here.

His brother's call was strong. Golden Eyes was no more than a mile away now. Red Eyes could smell him, and it was not altogether an unpleasant smell. His feelings betrayed him. He allowed himself to be joyful, for a moment, at Miguel's scent. Then he hardened again and pushed his emotions away. They would not serve him well right now. He had to be strong, to resist decades of familial ties and responsibilities. He had to push aside those weak, human tendencies. He had to focus on the matter at hand: reaching Golden Eyes and…

He dropped the poodle façade and moved now in his true form, the form he had worn for almost two centuries. The form his brother wore as well. There was no need for subterfuge or deception now. His brother awaited, and soon they would be reunited.

Red Eyes followed the strong scent forward through trimmed backyards and over quiet streets. He did not shine his red eyes at anyone this time and drive them mad; he had no time for that now, nor did he need the additional strength. He was as strong as he had ever been, and it was sufficient for anything his brother or that woman might throw at him. Red Eyes breathed deeply and howled.

I'm on my way, little brother. I'm on my way.

The location Golden Eyes had chosen surprised him. It seemed so insignificant, so basic and uninspiring. No grandiose mountains in the background, no violent cataracts nearby to freshen the air with their whitewater foam. But then, Miguel had always been that way in human life: small, discarded, weak. There was a certain irony in choosing a junkyard for their reunion, he supposed, for they were both discarded creatures in a way, two cursed boys who had tricked an old magician and wound up paying the ultimate price. Two pieces of junk, forgotten and shunned by human society.

Red Eyes entered the junkyard. He trotted through the puddles of mud, twisting and turning through piles of metal trash, some choked with weeds and rusty barbed wire. The place was filthy. Rain clouds peppered the sky. The air was lousy with moldy smells of oil and rotting rubber tires, and—

There he was. Miguel. Golden Eyes, sitting in front of the largest pile of cars, patient as if merely there to sun himself. Quiet, unassuming, calm.

Hello, Isai, Golden Eyes said, raising a hoof in salutation.

Red Eyes raised his hoof. *Hello, Miguel.*

"Stop!"

Father de Seña, who was driving, almost hit a pedestrian as he slammed on the brakes and brought their van to a sliding halt. He punched it into *park* and said, crossing his chest, "Forgive me, Father, but damn you, Chimalis! What's the matter with you? I almost hit that man."

It was the strongest sensation that she had felt yet in her moves to shadow *El Cadejo.* Golden Eyes spoke directly to her, guiding her to where they needed to go. He was letting her see the world through his eyes.

"Let me drive," she said, pushing Father de Seña hard against his door. "I know where they are."

Father de Seña resisted. "We're going to Our Lady of Guadalupe for your protection, Chimalis. Remember? You have to receive the sacrament to be protected. If we're dealing with the devil here, we—"

"No time for that, Father!" She felt like smacking him but stayed her hand. "They are meeting now."

"I can drive," Luiz said, holding up his hand rather sheepishly from the back seat. "If you two have things to discuss before—"

"Let me drive!" She screamed at Father de Seña and then immediately felt bad about it. But the sensation in her mind, with Miguel showing her the way through his beautiful, radiant eyes, would not subside. There was no time for the sacrament, no time for spiritual protection. Whatever happened would happen. Now was the time.

Father de Seña sighed, crossed his chest again, then got out. Chimalis slid into the driver's seat, adjusted it and the rearview mirror, then strapped in. Father de Seña came around to the other side of the car and got back in. "This is a mistake, Chimalis. Your father would not be happy with you risking yourself like this."

No, he wouldn't, she wanted to say but held her tongue. *That's why he failed to get them in El Salvador. He hesitated. Why, I don't know. But I won't. I'll put an end to what he could not.*

Slowly, she turned the car around and guided it through the mass of crazed pedestrians running and screaming and committing all acts of violence. Chimalis could barely keep her mind on the road as she tried not to hit anyone.

She shook her head at the madness on display in the streets of Lubbock. All because of a dog with goat hooves and small horns. All because of two selfish boys who couldn't fetch a few lousy chunks of firewood for an old man.

All because of *El Cadejo.*

"It has been too long," Miguel said, yipping to accentuate his meaning. "How have you been?"

"Surviving," Isai said, responding in kind but wasting no time. "You abandoned me, Miguel. I looked up, and you were gone."

Miguel shook himself. The dust of the road billowed from his thick fur. "No. You went too far, Isai. I couldn't endure so much death and despair anymore. You stopped caring, and when you did that, everything around you fell to pieces. I could not allow that to happen to me."

Isai moved closer. Miguel countered by moving away. They circled each other around a sizeable mud puddle, sirens wailing in the distance. "You left me to suffer the privations of the citizenry. I could go nowhere without constant persecution. Without you there, to be my scout, I could not travel into any area without falling into their traps. I almost died thrice, Miguel, because you weren't there."

Circling and circling. "Funny," Miguel said, snorting the word through his thoughts, "but I don't recall you ever placing such importance on my presence in your life, big brother. You were the smart one, the clever one. You never let me forget it."

"I've changed, Miguel. Thirty years on my own. I see the light now."

Miguel paused his circling. "So, you wish to reconcile? To 'bury the hatchet,' as humans say? To be a good brother for once?"

Isai paused, shook himself. "No. We must do now what we should have done right after that despicable magician turned us into freaks."

"You did him wrong, Isai. He asked for a simple chore to be done for his hospitality, and you betrayed him."

Circling and circling. "I betrayed him? You were there too, brother, or do you forget?"

Miguel snorted in anger. "I remember every moment of it, damn you. Every day, every hour. I should have fetched the wood myself, and to hell with you. I should have let you burn alone and forever in this hellish curse that we have both been confined to."

"Ah, but you didn't, did you, sweet brother? You allowed yourself to be bullied, by me, like you have always done."

Miguel paused, growled. "Not anymore."

He leapt over the puddle toward Isai, who caught him in the brisket, rolled, and flung him aside with his hind hooves like a discarded bone. Miguel slid across the soft ground, leaving a trail of hoof marks in his wake. "Don't you want to wait until your girlfriend arrives? She's on her way, with her priest buddy."

"A priest?" Miguel recovered, stood, shook off the mud, said quickly to mask his fear, "Have you been quoting Revelations again, Isai?"

Isai's chuckle sounded like he was choking on a hairball. He sneezed and said, "It's been useful over the years to convince the gullible that I am Satan. It keeps the religiously-inclined reminded of their role in our fall from grace."

Miguel moved cautiously toward Isai, and they began to circle again. "They've had no role in any of this. We were cursed by an ex-slave of West African descent. God has played no role."

Isai snorted, howled. "God's people created *De Bibliis Maledictione*, codifying the curse that has confined us to this horrible fate. They are at the very center of our affliction. They must all see what they have wrought. They must be here to witness the end."

"Are you going to kill me, Isai? Your own brother?"

Isai paused, yipped. "I'm going to kill everyone."

Chimalis had been picking up bits and pieces of the brothers' conversation as she sped toward their location. It came through her mind like a garbled radio transmission. It was one of the most annoying sensations that she had ever felt in her career. But as she drew closer, and as she whipped the car into the dirt-and-gravel parking lot of the junkyard, with FBI backup blaring sirens behind them, two important details became clear.

First, Red Eyes was not Satan. That was a relief. It meant that Father de Seña's presence was not needed, though she knew he would refuse to stay in the car. Nor would he necessarily believe what *El Cadejo* had conveyed to her through her mind. Satan was a cagey beast, Father de Seña would say. The Prince of Lies. So, she did not tell him that nugget of good news. It would do no good anyway.

Second, the brothers had not come together to join forces. That had been pretty clear for a while now, but again, in her line of work, it never hurt to confirm the matter once and for all. They had come to fight each other.

Chimalis slid the van to a halt. "Louie," she said, "I want you to stay with Father de Seña and keep him safe. Keep him back from the danger zone while I—"

"You're going to need me close, Chimalis," Father de Seña said, allowing Luiz to help him out of the car. "If this thing is Satan, you're gonna—"

"Please, Father," she said, slamming the car door shut. "Please trust me. Stay back, and I promise you, if I need your assistance, you'll know. But this is for me to do, not you. Please trust me!"

Father de Seña rolled his eyes, and Chimalis could see the fear in them, the fear for her life. Her soul. She could tell that, if things went bad for her, Father de Seña would blame himself. "Okay, girl. I'll stay back. But if you get killed, I swear I'll resurrect you just to kill you myself."

Chimalis smiled as sincerely as possible. She pulled the Zuni ritual knife from her purse and snapped it to her belt. "We have a deal."

Isai perked his long ears. "Ah, very good. She has arrived." The blare of sirens drew even closer. "And she's brought all her friends. Shall we finally show her what really happened at El Mozote? Shall I tell her?"

Miguel nodded and raised his hoof. "You tell her your side of it, then I'll tell her the truth."

She fell to the ground and gripped her head. The images of El Mozote forced into her mind were strong, very strong, almost too strong to endure. They were stark and clear as if she had been there.

"They've got a wolf." A government soldier of the Atlacatl Battalion said to his superior when he had returned from the village. "They've got it in a cage."

"What are they gonna do," his commander asked, "cook it?"

A laugh. "I don't know. But it's pretty banged up. Bloody, weak, as if they had beaten it up real good before locking it away.

Looks like they might sacrifice it to a Mayan god or something to keep us away. Looks like they fear that wolf more than us."

More laughter. "They may do what they will with it. Just so long as they keep inside and not come out. That's all we ask."

Red Eyes, shaped in the illusion of a common German Shepard, was lying in the corner, listening intently to everything these despicable men were saying. *They've got Miguel, and he's injured, perhaps near death. I warned him not to go to the villagers. He never listens, never...*

The fear of Miguel dying now overwhelmed him. The fear of being alone, to roam the world in this cursed state forever without a friend, someone to rely on, without Miguel, without a brother... was too much. Too much to endure.

Red Eyes felt real fear, real danger, for the first time in this life. He panicked and revealed his true self to the soldiers. They were shocked, of course, but Red Eyes made it clear what they must do. Dawn was near, the sun was rising, and there was only one way to ensure that Miguel was freed from his prison. Only one way, the only solution left to him by the magician on that warm, foggy morning in Eighteen Forty-Five.

Within an hour, the killing began as the villagers were taken out of their homes: men, women, children, all lined up and shot. Anger and abject rage spread through the government soldiers like a fire, and there was no stopping them now, and Red Eyes was loath to do so. *They almost took my brother from me. They must pay the price.*

Miguel was found, freed, and saved. The killing continued through the morning, but what did it matter? *My brother was free,* Red Eyes said. *Miguel will live.*

"Are you okay, boss?" Luiz asked, trying to help Chimalis to her feet. "Perhaps we shouldn't do this. Let the fellows with the guns deal with them."

"No, no," she said, clearing her mind, standing, and reaching for the knife at her belt. "I'm okay. Let's go."

She took three steps and fell to the ground.

Chapter Ten

Again, she was in El Salvador, right outside the village of El Mozote, and she was staring into the eyes of a drunk.

A foolish, arrogant young man who had ignored the Atlacatl Battalion's order to stay home, to stay inside. He had stepped out with a friend and was now stumbling back home, and Golden Eyes found him and escorted him safely to his village. His duty to protect the weak, the inebriated, wasn't something that Golden Eyes could ignore. He had to help, even if he didn't want to.

Once there, however, Golden Eyes realized the potential danger of the villagers as they, albeit quietly, secretly defied the government's wishes. Golden Eyes understood their position. The El Salvadoran government has been brutal with these people, and perhaps Golden Eyes could help them.

He revealed himself to them in full, no veil, no deception. A mistake, and he realized it immediately, but what was done was done. The villagers ambush him, and he tried to explain to them that he was there to help, to protect them, but the legend of *El Cadejo* had spread far and wide, and no amount of explanation would sway these people into believing that Golden Eyes was actually there to help. He was there on behalf of the government. No, he tried telling them. His brother, Isai, was moving with the Atlacatl Battalion. *He is the one you should fear.* But they were terrified, and they saw no distinction between the two; one in the same.

The villagers attacked and beat him, but he did not resist. He let them throw him in a cage, and through his suffering, perhaps they would realize that he was there to help. All he wanted to do was to help.

And then the massacre began, and Golden Eyes knew that the government forces were working under his brother's command. Killing and killing and killing until there is no one left to kill.

In time, Red Eyes found and freed his brother, but Golden Eyes had had enough. There is no thanks, no praise or gratitude for Isai. Just anger… anger and sadness.

Despite the pain and suffering that the villagers had heaped upon him, Golden Eyes found the strength to leap from the cage. He ran and ran and ran and never looked back, despite Red Eyes calling him to stop, to go no further. Golden Eyes did not stop running until his brother's commands and the hate he exuded, could no longer be felt or heard.

"Chimalis!" Luiz shows anger and worry in his voice. "Enough of this. Let us retreat. You cannot handle this. It's too strong for you. Please."

"I'm okay now," she said, standing again and taking comfort in Luiz's grip. "It's over now. They've told me the whole story. I understand everything. Let's go."

She and Luiz and Father de Seña moved forward, into the junkyard and in view of the brothers.

"You killed those people for me?" Miguel could not believe it and shook his head in disgust. "You lie!"

Isai shook his head. "No, it is true. I thought they were going to kill you."

"They were afraid, Isai! Afraid of me, afraid of the armed men inside their village. Afraid of everything."

"And they were going to kill you because of it."

"So what!"

There it was. The truth that Miguel had not even admitted to himself. The truth that, in some small way, he had wanted them to kill him. Wanted them to finish him off after a hundred and forty years of wandering aimlessly through a world of human beings but never being able to act like one, like he and Isai used to do in their youth. He was bound to protect that drunk, yes, but once there, he could have simply left, clopped away to let the situation evolve as it may. But no. He had stayed, and staying had brought death to them, not him.

No! He said to himself. *I do this all the time. I let Isai manipulate me into blaming myself. No. Not anymore.*

"But then you left anyway," Isai said, scratching the soft ground with his hoof. "I freed you, and you ran," Isai lowered his head. "I was alone anyway."

"And then you ordered the battalion to conduct other massacres, didn't you?"

Isai said nothing at first. Then he stopped scratching the ground, raised his head, and stared into Miguel's eyes. "What else could I do, but try to fill the space you left empty?"

And now, an anger that Miguel had never felt before rose into his throat. The death of all those innocent people, from all those senseless massacres, that his brother had caused helped propel him over the mud puddle and slam into Isai with full force.

Chimalis heard the sounds of their battle even before she rounded the corner and saw them. There they were: two large grey wolves, bearing hooves and horns, tearing into each other with a violence that she could not only see but feel. Father de Seña leaned on her, grabbed her arm for support. "Please, Chimalis," the priest said. "Don't get involved."

It was too late for that. The brothers themselves had made it impossible for her to just sit back and watch. They had invited her into their lives, had given her a taste of how it had been to live twisted, confused, and in pain, for almost two hundred years. She was like their sister now.

"Hold him back, Louie," she said as her partner held the priest in support. "This is my show."

"Chimalis…." Luiz called to her, but she didn't listen. She held her knife forward, which now glowed hot with all the spirits of its previous kills. It longed to vanquish another, and she would oblige it, if she could just get close enough.

But which one to strike, and how could she do it without being driven mad by Red Eyes or even by Golden Eyes in the throes of rage and volatility? Red Eyes was the most lethal, and obviously, the most critical to see vanquished.

She drew closer as the sirens of her arriving backup subsided. Car doors opened, orders barked. A line of FBI agents, supported by a SWAT assault team, came into view and encircled the danger zone. Guns raised, shields and riot gear ready.

Chimalis raised her hand to the officers. "Steady," she said, trying not to be too loud as to alert the brothers to how close she had drawn. "Do nothing unless I order it."

Isai felt the tear of flesh across his shoulder. Miguel had sunk his fangs into a vulnerable place and bitten down hard. Isai howled and kicked Miguel away with his back hooves. His brother slid across the mud but stopped quickly and leapt again. Isai took the attack in his throat, and they both fell into the center of the muddy puddle.

Isai's snout went below the foul water. He gasped for air. *Miguel's not playing,* he thought, as he held his breath to keep from choking on mud. *He's trying to kill me.*

For the first time in decades, Isai felt sorrow, and for once, he didn't know what to do. With his strength and size, he could easily toss Miguel aside and then hit him with insurmountable force. *I can break his neck with one bite and toss him aside like a doll.* But did he want to do that?

Amidst feelings of sorrow, he also felt pride. Finally, at long last, his little brother had shown some spine, some strength and determination. Miguel was serious now, and all of his anger and timidity had fused into one violent rush of attack.

To make it look good, Isai lashed out and kicked Miguel aside, sending him into a pile of trash. He then rose out of the mud and stood there, quiet, ready, knowing that the woman with a tiny blade in her hand drew very close now. He turned to her and flashed his red eyes.

She ducked and covered her face, letting the glow of his stare reflect off the blade in her hand and dissipate harmlessly in the humid air.

Isai thought about leaping toward her, finishing her off with one quick bite before she had time to recover, but Miguel slammed into him again and pushed him further into the mud.

Now his own rage took over. Isai was finished letting Miguel have his playtime. He had not come all the way here to wallow in mud; he'd come here to do what should have been done decades ago.

Isai kicked Miguel away once more. Then he attacked, sinking his large teeth into his brother's throat and clamping down with a bite that had, in the past, broken the necks of jaguars. Miguel's hide, however, was just as tough and resilient as his own, and so the bite did not bring death, though Isai could hear and feel his brother's neck bones grind as they slammed into each other like ice in a glass. Miguel howled and jammed his hooves into Isai's soft underbelly, ripping into the stomach and letting blood flow.

Isai bit harder and tasted blood, a shower of it as his fangs ripped through Miguel's jugular. Miguel yelped and struggled against the bite, driving his hoof deeper and deeper into Isai's bowel. *Yes, yes*, Isai thought, feeling his brother's hoof slice through the lining of his stomach and into his intestines.

With Miguel's throat still clamped between his teeth, Isai rose out of the mud and growled triumphantly. He was so happy. Overjoyed. For the first time since the curse, he felt relief, as if a crushing weight had been lifted from his soul.

"Together," Isai said so that Miguel could hear it through his mind, "we will see death. Together, we will—"

Isai felt a *thunk!* and a sharp sting in his back. He dropped Miguel and slowly, slowly, turned to see what had struck him.

Chapter Eleven

Chimalis had never thrown the knife before. She had always gotten close enough to her baddies to drive it right in with force and certainty. She had no choice this time. Red Eyes had his brother by the throat, and if she hadn't acted immediately, Golden Eyes would have died, and Red Eyes might have slipped away.

It wasn't until she moved closer that she realized Isai was going nowhere either with Miguel's hoof buried deep into his bowel.

She moved closer as the knife sticking out of Red Eyes' back pulsed yellow, then orange, then red, as it accepted the tortured spirit within the collapsing body of the grey wolf. Chimalis stopped and stared at Red Eyes' massive canine form, as it reacted to the blade and shrank before her eyes, becoming smaller and smaller until there was no wolf left. Only the frail, emaciated body of a mulatto boy remained.

Chimalis reached down and pulled the knife free. She knelt beside them both. Foolish, perhaps, to risk such exposure, but the curse was gone, at least for Isai. Chimalis stared deeply into the boy's bruised, gaunt face. She looked him straight in the eyes. Nothing. No madness or anger filled her mind. She felt nothing but sorrow and disappointment. Not for doing what she had to do; this was her job. No. She felt sorrow because before her now was nothing but a frail little boy, almost comical in his thinness, with his guts hanging out of his stomach, his life draining away. Had he deserved such a curse simply for refusing to fetch a pile of wood? Did anyone deserve such treatment?

Miguel began to change as well. Not as fast as Isai due to the draining powers of the knife, but slowly his fur began to recede, his snout shrank by inches, and his long wolfen spine began to twist and turn until all that was left was a smaller version of Isai. Another little boy who did not deserve his fate.

They stared at each other, Isai bleeding out at his stomach, Miguel at his throat. Isai reached for Miguel across the muddy water. Miguel reached out as well. Their hands touched.

Chimalis stepped away.

"Is this what you wanted, Isai?" Miguel asked, for the first time in almost two centuries, moving his own mouth, speaking Spanish. It felt good. "To die like this?"

"Together?" Isai nodded as blood trickled out from the wound in his stomach. "I cannot live in this world without you, brother. And I dare to think that perhaps you cannot live without me as well. And so, would you have wanted it any other way?"

Miguel coughed and shook his head. Blood drained down his chest from the bite mark in his throat. "No. This was the only way." Tears began to run down his face. "I'm sorry, Isai. I should have been stronger in those woods. I should have stood up to you. I could have fetched that wood myself. I wanted to, but I—I—"

Isai shook his head and squeezed his brother's hand tightly. "No, Miguel. For once, let me take the blame. It was my fault. We are here because of me, not you. El Mozote was my fault, El Calabozo, El Paraiso, and a thousand other smaller massacres. All my fault. You share no blame for any of it. Do you understand?"

He did, and he nodded slowly. "Goodbye, Isai. I love you, brother."

Tears ran down Isai's messy face. "I love you… brother."

And then he was gone.

Miguel could live. His wound was deep and dangerous, but not necessarily lethal. Chimalis had seen wounds like it before. All he needed was something to stop the blood flow, a strong compress, a clamp, a—

"Come, now, Chimalis," Miguel said to her. He motioned with a weak hand. "Come, and end this."

"But you can be saved."

"No," he said, blurting out the words in a gout of blood. "Take the knife and finish me."

It was the right thing to do, but Chimalis lost her nerve. Why was she balking? *Pick up the knife and end this, forever.*

She picked up the knife. It was warm, and the handle now had a small, firelit icon of *El Cadejo*, but only half. She had to finish it now, or the icon would always be half-formed and incomplete.

"Your father would have been proud of you, Chimalis."

She froze, the knife still in her hand. She looked at Miguel. "You knew my father?"

He nodded. "Yes. I wasn't sure if you were his daughter, but it's clear to me now that you are. You have his eyes, his spirit. He almost had Isai at *Sumpul* River, a year before El Mozote, but I stopped him. I stopped him because I couldn't live in a world without my brother, to roam forever by myself, trapped between the world of man and beast. Isai can take the blame if he wants, but the blame is mine. I was never strong enough to stand up to him. I am the cause of all of this. You must end this, now, Chimalis. Please."

She knelt beside him. She ran her hand over his face and closed his eyelids. She whispered a Zuni prayer, modifying it on the fly to fit the moment.

"Your days are past, and let the road of your wandering end, and go now to that place where all roads end and life may begin anew, in the spirit shadow of the sun."

She drove the knife into his side. Miguel let out a small breath, then smiled as the blade glowed hot and accepted his spirit. His body shook, and then he was gone.

"Ugh! What's that ghastly smell?"

Luiz and Father de Seña had come up behind her. She waited until Miguel's body had, like Isai's, dissolved into dust and then pulled the blade away. She looked at the hilt. The *El Cadejo* icon was now complete.

She smiled, wiggled her nose, and said, "I guess it's from decades of corruption and evil acts. The Mapuche demons smelled pretty bad too when they died."

Luiz shook his head and whistled. "Nothing like this, though, I imagine."

Chimalis couldn't argue with him. The scent that the brothers had left behind seemed nearly life-threatening, and they all moved away quickly to get out from under its staggering miasma. There was no reason to linger anyway. There would be no forensics team inbound to survey the site. This was a conclusion to a paranormal investigation. Chimalis would return to Denver, write up her report, and check her knife into VPA Tech to get it cleared for future action. That was all.

"Are you okay, girl?" Father de Seña placed his hand on her shoulder.

Was she? The physical and psychological toll of a paranormal investigation was often difficult to endure, and many VPA agents couldn't handle it. This assignment was not as physically draining as she had anticipated, but the emotional toll... the anguish of the brothers, the decades of misunderstanding between them, the foolish pride and false blame that had brought them to this place, had threatened to overwhelm her. Even now, with them gone and their combined spirits vanquished by her Zuni ritual blade, they called to her. Like family. She was their sister. And how long would this feeling last?

"I'll be fine," she said, forcing a smile. "Eventually. Let's get out of here."

"Where to now, boss?" Luiz asked as they reached their van.

Chimalis' stomach growled. "Lunch. Your treat. And then... I'm taking a fucking vacation!"

About the Author

Robert E Waters is a technical writer by trade, but has been a science fiction/fantasy fan all his life. He's worked in the computer and board gaming industry since 1994 as designer, producer, and writer. In the late 90's, he tried his hand at writing fiction, and since 2003, has sold over 7 novels and 80 stories to various on-line and print magazines and anthologies, including the *Grantville Gazette*, Eric Flint's online magazine dedicated to publishing stories set in the 1632/Ring of Fire Alternate History series.

Robert's first 1632/Ring of Fire novel, *1636: Calabar's War*, (co-authored with Charles E Gannon), was recently published by Baen Books. Robert has also co-written several 1632 stories, including the *Persistence of Dreams* (Ring of Fire Press), with Meriah L Crawford, and *The Monster Society*, with Eric S Brown.

Robert is the author of *The Mask Cycle*, a Baroque fantasy series which includes the novels *The Masks of Mirada* and *The Thief of Cragsport* (Ring of Fire Press).

For e-Spec Books, Robert has written several stories which have appeared in the widely popular military science fiction anthology series, *Defending the Future*. All seven of his stories which appeared in the series were recently collected into one volume titled *Devil Dancers*.

Robert currently lives in Baltimore, Maryland with his wife Beth, their son Jason, and their two precocious little cats, Snow and Ashe.

artist's rendition of El Cadejo

EL CADEJO

(From the Spanish word *"cadena"* meaning "chain.")

ORIGINS: A creature, or at times two creatures, cited in Central American folklore, primarily that of El Salvador, Belize, Costa Rica, Nicaragua, Honduras, Guatemala, and southern Mexico.

While their origin is claimed to be the result of a curse in most accounts, there are multiple variations. In the vast majority of those, there are always two *cadejo*: one white and one black. The white one is said to be benevolent, protecting those out late at night, particularly drunks. The black one is malicious, harrying and even harming travelers not by direct attack, but by driving them mad. There are some regional accounts where the natures of the *cadejo* are reversed, with the black being good and the white evil.

In other variations, there are said to be three types of black *cadejo*. The first is the very embodiment of the devil, appearing as a large, wounded dog with smoldering chains about its hooved feet. Rather than do harm, this one is a harbinger of misfortune.

The second variation is a vicious black dog that torments its victims before tearing into them, unless the white *cadejo* is nearby.

The final variation is the offspring of a normal dog and a black *cadejo*. This one can be killed, though with difficulty, and it does not savage its victims, but drives them mad with eerie sounds and by pounding them with its muzzle.

As mentioned, the origins of this cryptid seem rooted in myth and legend, but it bears noting that mankind has a long history of creating tall tales to explain natural occurences, and despite the supposed magical nature of these beasts, there have been more current reports of sightings.

DESCRIPTION: In most accounts, the *cadejo* are paired, one white beast and one black, but sometimes there is just one, and if so, that one is the black *cadejo*. They have the appearance of wolves or dogs, but can be anything from normal size to as big as a cow, with the horns and hooves of goats, or in some accounts, bulls. They are said to smell either strongly of goat, or like the stench of urine combined with sulphur. Some say that they have burning red eyes, or that the black *cadejo* is red-eyed, and the white *cadejo* is either blue-, green-, or golden-eyed. It is believed that if you meet their gaze, you will be unable to move.

Life Cycle: though some regions believe it is possible for *cadejo* to breed with common dogs, details on their development remain unavailable. It is noted that such offspring bear a similar demeanor to their cryptid parent, as well as being nearly as difficult to kill. When one has been dispatched, the body puts off a foul odor before dissolving into nothing, leaving behind a stain on the earth from which nothing will grow thenceforth.

History: The most common legend of *el cadejo* speaks of two brothers traveling through the wilderness. They stop at the home of a black magician. In exchange for food and a place to stay the night, they agree to collect wood for the magician's fire. In the morning, when the man sees that they didn't not honor their agreement, he casts a curse upon them as they leave, harrying them with voices and sounds until they turn away, then changing them into beasts according to their nature. Thus cursed, they are cast out from their home and forced to wander, driven by the curse to help or harm travelers.

To this day, truckers have reported these cryptids along the highways up through Texas, and there are *el cadejo* sightings as far as the hills of Lake Elsinore, in Southern California.

About the Artist

Although Jason Whitley has worn many creative hats, he is at heart a traditional illustrator and painter. With author James Chambers, Jason collaborates and illustrates the sometimes-prose, sometimes graphic novel, *The Midnight Hour,* which is being collected into one volume by eSpec Books. His and Scott Eckelaert's newspaper comic strip, Sea Urchins, has been collected into four volumes. Along with eSpec Books' Systema Paradoxa series, Jason is working on a crime noir graphic novel. His portrait of Charlotte Hawkins Brown is on display in the Charlotte Hawkins Brown Museum.

CAPTURE THE CRYPTIDS!

Cryptid Crate is a monthly subscription box filled with various cryptozoology and paranormal themed items to wear, display and collect. Expect a carefully curated box filled with creeptastic pieces from indie makers and artisans pertaining to bigfoot, sasquatch, UFOs, ghosts, and other cryptid and mysterious creatures (apparel, decor, media, etc).

http://CryptidCrate.com